A Road less travelled

The Mysore Triology, Volume 1

R RADHAKRISHNAN

Published by Radhakrishnan R, 2023.

A ROAD LESS TRAVELLED

First edition. May 24, 2023.

Copyright © 2023 R RADHAKRISHNAN.

ISBN: 979-8223582380

Written by R RADHAKRISHNAN.

Also by R RADHAKRISHNAN

The Mysore Triology
A Road less travelled

The Temples of India
The Temples of India: Somnathapura, Mysore

Travellers Tales
Rustic Romeo

Standalone
The Colors of Life
The Temples of India : Guruvayur
Indian Mythology
The Book of Ancient Wisdom
Karna's Song
Artificial intelligence : AI for writers

Table of Contents

Prologue..1

Chapter one 3

Chapter two...5

Chapter three...8

Chapter four 13

Chapter five...16

Chapter six 19

Chapter seven 21

Chapter eight..23

Chapter nine...31

Chapter ten 35

Chapter eleven 39

Chapter twelve 42

Chapter thirteen 47

Chapter fourteen 53

Chapter fifteen 57

Chapter sixteen 61

Chapter seventeen 64

Chapter eighteen 68

Chapter nineteen 70

Chapter twenty 75

Chapter twenty one 78

Epilogue...82

To

Ganesha

&

My kids, Aishwariya and Avaneesh, may you always chase your
dreams and find happiness.

Prologue

Somewhere in the Indian Ocean:

I stood at the rail of my ship, INS Mysore, the Indian Navy's guided missile destroyer.

We expected to make landfall early morning the next day at Cochin. I was due for a spot of leave.

I looked at the messages on my phone; they were expecting me to be there for the wedding of my brother.

Cochin appeared on the horizon early morning and I was at the rail watching the dawn appear over this beautiful city.

I disembarked and there on shore stood Prasanna, my closest friend. He smiled when he saw me in my dress whites.

"So Krish, you have achieved your dream and become a naval officer, looking good, man."

I laughed. "What brings you here? Have you been transferred?" I asked.

"No, I came to see you, you idiot. I know you will avoid coming back to Mysore. It has been two years. We all miss you Krish. Why don't you come for a few days, at least attend the marriage? Raghu and your parents told me they had called and pleaded with you, but you had refused. I thought to come and try to talk some sense into you."

I laughed. "I wanted to attend the marriage and see all of you, but they have selected me for the Antarctica Mission and I have to be in Delhi by tomorrow," I evaded. "You know Prasanna how important this is to me,"

"More important than your family and friends, Krish," he asked.

"Don't say that. I have missed all of you. I still remember the fun we had you, me, Bhavna, Veena and Govind," I replied.

"And Snehlata, do you remember her?" He asked "and your mother, father and brother," do you miss them?

I shrugged and smiled crookedly. "They will be there when I return. This is a once in a lifetime opportunity which I cannot miss."

He looked at me, resigned to my obstinate refusal. "Well, I tried, but you were always a headstrong chap, anyway I am glad I could see you, my friend," he said.

I laughed; "hey you were always more obstinate than me. Honestly, I just want to go on this mission. There is no other motive."

He looked skeptical, but let it go. Our friendship was like that. We never judged each other and accepted each other as we were.

We spent the day together going around the bazar area of Fort Kochi. I took him to meet my Naval friends, and we also caught up on each other.

We traveled to the airport in the evening. He to catch his flight to Bangalore and from there go to Mysore and me to Delhi to report for my mission to Antarctica.

I leaned back in my seat for the long flight to Delhi. My thoughts wandered to the events two years back...

Chapter one

She had large eyes that gazed at you expressionless, in her oval face, long black hair tied in an untidy knot and a pencil dangling from her slender fingers.

She wore no makeup and my first impression was of a woman of confidence, a no-nonsense person who neither needed nor brooked any frills.

She was the lead architect in the firm and I had come to check with her regarding the structural drawings for our new office.

As I stood there, tongue tied, she lifted her eyebrows in query. Luckily, Govind, their coordinator for our project, stepped into the breech.

"Krishnan is from the Indian Logistics Company Limited Sneha. He is executive assistant to Raghu Nandan," said Govind.

She looked at me and what she saw was a slim young man, little over medium height, rather curly hair, large dark eyes, a cleft chin and a ready smile.

"Oh, well, what do you want?" she asked, a bit brusquely ignoring my smile. I gulped and stammered, "we were to get the draft plans this morning so that we could go over it and freeze the plan. We want to start the work by next week."

She snorted with irritation and said, "you tell Raghu it is not possible. I had clarified that I need more time to make proper plans and drawings. We are not machines where you punch data and get the output."

I waited, but she turned back to the drawing she was working on. I cleared my throat, and she turned back to me. "Is there anything else?" she asked.

I stammered again, "I cannot tell him that. He will be upset. Please let me know when we can expect the plans?"

She waved her hand dismissively and turned back to her drawing. I was annoyed and upset. Raghu had a habit of ripping up at small things. This would invite a storm and he would believe I had not tried to get the plan.

"Ma'am, at least have the courtesy to reply to me. We are paying you for this. It is not free."

She turned slowly and smiled at me, and I lost my anger. "The child is angry," she said.

I flushed and replied, "I am no child".

"OK, young man," she smiled that captivating smile again, "Tell that fat Raghu that the plans will be ready by Saturday, you can come and pick them up by around 1 pm." and she turned back to her drawing board.

Govind was wiping his brow "For a minute I thought Sneha would rip you apart. She has a short fuse."

"How do you guys tolerate her?" I asked. "Oh, she is a lovely and charming woman normally, it is only when she is working and focused on something, she is like this," replied Govind.

"But she is a genius and even the bosses don't disturb her," he said. "She joined us around six months back. She does not really have to work. Her father is a big business person in Mumbai."

Chapter two

I reached back to the office and walked into the CEO's secretariat. We were a large all India logistics company based out of our hometown of Mysore. Our trucks that carried a variety of goods all over India.

Many of the trucks were on contract. Our own trucks were only about forty percent of the fleet of trucks we operated.

Our own trucks mostly moved on fixed routes as we had long-term contracts with leading white goods manufacturers, two-wheeler and four-wheeler manufacturers, and we had dedicated fleets for each of these customers.

In Mysore, TVS had their two-wheeler manufacturing and were our biggest customers. There were other industries also who were our customers and our business was booming thanks to the single-minded focus of Raghu Nandan, our founder, and managing director.

I slipped into Raghu's room and he turned around from the window from which he was gazing into the horizon. He turned, and I hesitantly told him that their lead architect had said that we could have the plans by the coming Saturday. He nodded dismissal and went back to his horizon gazing.

I wondered at the calm; I had expected he would blow his top, call me a useless idiot and call up the Architects to shout at them as well.

It was lunchtime and promptly at 1 pm Raghu came out and we walked back together to our house at the back. Raghu was my elder brother, almost six years my senior, a hard driven, no-nonsense person. He was a stocky, well-built man with determination writ all over him. It was there in his eyes as he looked at you, sizing you up. His walk was brisk., his speech was short and many a time sharp. He was a man in a hurry.

He ruffled my hair as we went inside the house, grinning at me. I took courage in my hands to ask him, "do you think they will give us the drawing on Saturday?".

"If Snehlata has said they will give, it will be ready," he replied.

I looked at him in wonder. "You know her?".

He looked up. "Yes, she was there during the discussions we had with their fir."

We sat at the table, and Amma came to serve us.

"Oh, she has met you," I asked. "She said tell that fat Raghu," I grinned at him.

He smiled back, "yeah, I have put on some weight in the past few months. Guess I need to go more regularly for my badminton game,"

My mother was silent, but she was not pleased anyone criticizing her elder son.

Lunch was a quick and brief affair and we were soon back at the office. My brother made up for his earlier pleasantness by being an absolute despot till the late evening.

The next few days sped by quickly. There seemed to be no time for anything other than work.

My father protested to my mother, "Satya, the kid has just come a couple of months back from Pondicherry after his MBA. Let him have a look around before settling down."

My brother laughed. "What do you think he was doing those two years in Pondicherry? They have a very easy course and he would have spent all his time in lazing around and drinking,"

My father laughed back "yes you would know better, having done the same thing when you were doing your MBA in Mumbai, you could have got admission to IIM Bangalore and or any other college in Mysore or Bangalore but you wanted to do only in Mumbai!"

My brother laughed. "No, I went to Mumbai because it was the business hub of India and I wanted to learn."

"Oh," said my father, "then what was the time you spent in Namakkal all about?"

"That was different. I wanted to learn more about the trucking business, and see where we have reached in the last five years. We are among the top in India and the biggest in South India," said my brother.

"But are you happy, my son?" asked my father gently, and Raghu turned away. "Leave him be Hari," said my mother. "He must be tired. Let him rest."

Chapter three

On Saturday my brother reminded me "you need to collect the drawings today and give it to me at lunchtime."

I nodded, but seeing me hesitate, Raghu raised his eyebrows. "I am planning to go for lunch with Prasanna and cannot join you for lunch today."

My brother nodded, and I went off doing my other chores.

I was well in time and as I kept chatting with Govind; I kept an eye out for Sneha. She breezed in a few minutes later, gave me a crooked smile, and went into her cabin.

My college buddy Prasanna walked in just as Sneha came out with the plans "We are not meeting to meet today, Prasanna" she said.

Prasanna smiled. "No Ma'am, I came to pick up Krish and Govind for lunch."

"Oh, you guys know each other,"? asked Sneha. "Yes, ma'am, we were together in college at Pondicherry, doing our MBA."

"Why don't you join us Sneha," said Govind. "You guys sure I will not be in the way? Sneha responded.

"No, come along," said Govind.

"What would you like to eat Ma'am" I asked politely as I tucked the plans inside my bags.

"We were planning to go to The Old House if that's OK with you," put in Govind.

"What's that," asked Sneha.

"A pizza joint," I answered. She shrugged and nodded. We stopped for a minute as I dropped off the plans in the office. My brother smiled. "Shall I come with you guys or will I cramp your style?"

I laughed at that. "Come, that architect has already joined us, so we will be on our best behavior," I said.

Raghu frowned. "Snehlata is joining you, then you carry on". I was surprised. My brother normally would have joined us and he liked both Prasanna and Govind.

"Why don't you like her" I asked. He smiled and shrugged; puzzled, I went down to join my friends.

The Old house was a popular place for the young and the young at heart. I just loved their Mushroom Bruschetta, their Mushroom Risotto and the Lasagna.

Sneha looked around the place and sighed. "I am happy I joined you guys; I was tired of the paying guest food I was having every day."

"Oh, Mysore has so many lovely places and such a variety of food that you should quite enjoy your stay here," I gushed.

Govind and Prasanna laughed at that. "Now you have set him off. He will bore us about the pleasures of Mysore," said Govind.

"Well, what do philistines from Pondicherry know," I replied.

"Hey machan, that's not fair, you also liked Pondicherry, specially that Qua-lithe bar and restaurant," laughed Govind.

I blushed, and Prasanna frowned at Govind. Prasanna was one of my closest friends, a serious career minded young man he did not like to open up in the presence of an outsider.

Sneha smiled, "don't be such hypocrites, you two. I too like to have a drink now and then."

The server came and took our orders and soon we were busy with our food and light-hearted conversation flowed among us.

I looked at Sneha; she was a few years elder than me, a fine-looking woman, not beautiful but full of life and charming when she wanted to be. Her nose was a bit long, I thought, and her teeth a bit crooked, a slender woman who exuded grace and class even in the faded jeans and off-white kurta she wore.

When the bill came, she took it over our protests to pay. Prasanna was quite upset. "Ma'am, you were just saying you believed in equality of the sexes, so let's not fight over this. We normally split the bills three ways. Today we will split it four ways."

Sneha smiled, "you are such a refreshing person, Prasanna; OK, we will split it four ways only if you consider me your friend and call me Sneha and not Ma'am. And don't you dare call me Didi."

Govind laughed "they will call you auntie, as you are always lecturing them."

"Guys, I had a wonderful time, thank you," said Sneha.

"Prasanna, Govind and me are meeting for dinner tonight with a couple of our other friends, Bhavna and Veena. Would you like to join?" I asked her.

"Well, if you guys don't mind an old lady's company," she smiled.

We met at the Habitat Mall in Jaylakshmipuram in the evening. Bhavna and Veena were there already with Prasanna, who would have picked them up as all the three stayed in nearby Gokulam.

In a few minutes Sneha arrived there with Govind, got introduced to Veena and Bhavna who were dentists doing their post-graduation in one of the well-known colleges in Mysore.

We did what we did on a Saturday; a little shopping by the girls mostly, a look at the various shops, decided not to see a movie and moved to have dinner at the Barbeque Nation restaurant inside the mall.

We found a table soon as they knew Prasanna at most of the upmarket restaurants, as he was the local field officer for a Petroleum Company, the largest in India. The company frequently had meetings, dinners and lunches for their customers and guests.

I hesitated ordering any liquor, but Sneha ordered tequila shots, Govind, Veena and Bhavna were having beer, Prasanna never touched liquor. I gave in and ordered my usual chilly vodka with soda instead of lemonade.

Sneha watched amused as I sipped the drink and said "the child drinks hard liquor".

Prasanna kept silent, keeping a vigilant eye on the barbecue on our table. The girls giggled and Govind laughed outright and said, "Sneha, he is our drinking champion. He loved Pondicherry because he loves to drink. He would drink everyone under the table."

I was embarrassed. "The trouble with you is that you talk too much, Govind," I said.

As the evening wore on, we became less inhibited and there was a lot of leg pulling and noise at our table. Only Prasanna sat, as usual, saying very little, smiling and watching Bhavna.

Bhavna, I noticed, was aware of the scrutiny and kept glancing at him. She and Veena were the vegetarians in our group and Prasanna ensured they were taken care of, as otherwise most of the barbecues would be meat.

Bhavna turned to Prasanna. "We are going to the bird sanctuary tomorrow, I hope." Prasanna nodded. Veena turned to Sneha saying, "why don't you join us? It will be fun and we can have lunch at the Barge later on."

"What's the Barge," asked Sneha. "Join us tomorrow and find out, as an architect, it will be interesting for you," invited Bhavna.

Govind excused himself he had to go meet some cousins who were coming from Coimbatore, so they asked me to pick up Sneha who had no vehicle of her own as of now.

"I hope you don't mind a two-wheeler; I do not have a car," I said. Prasanna looked at me quizzically. He knew I drove around in a Grand I10 belonging to Raghu most of the time.

But I wanted to have Sneha sit behind me on my 1976 Vintage Commando Norton motorcycle and also show it off to the girls. I wanted to get rid of the child tag, as both Bhavna and Veena seemed to find Sneha's comment hilarious; Veena kept referring to me as

"Kuzhanthai" which meant child in Tamil throughout the evening. I guess the vodka also went to my head a little.

Chapter four

The next day I turned up at Sneha's paying guest accommodation with my gleaming bike. She stepped out in her usual jeans and kurta top, with sneakers and her hair in a ponytail. But she still looked what she was, an elegant and graceful woman.

I handed over the spare helmet I had brought and she looked at motorcycle and then at me. "That's no child's toy there. I am impressed," she smiled.

We soon reached the ring road; Prasanna and the girls were meeting us at the entrance to the Ranganathittu Bird Sanctuary near Srirangapatna on the Cauvery.

I let the machine rip on the open road and forgot everything else in the wind's feel on my face and the beat of the engine. I slowed down as we entered the smaller roads and was soon at the gates of the sanctuary and parked beside Prasanna's car.

We removed our helmets, and I enjoyed the surprise on the girls' faces when they saw who it was. Veena was the first to recover. "Well well, who would have thought that Kuzhanthai had such a lovely toy, bought by big brother?" She asked maliciously. I reddened in anger and embarrassment.

Before I could say anything, Prasanna stepped in. "Veena, that motorcycle was a junk in Pondicherry when Krish bought it. He has restored it with a lot of hard work and dedication. Don't make fun of things you don't understand." I could see he was upset; I could also see that this could affect his relations with Bhavna if this continued. But Prasanna was like that. He would do anything for a friend and damn the consequences.

"Hey it is OK man, she is probably jealous as he took me on the bike," laughed Sneha and Veena blushed at that.

The moment passed, and we were soon on the Cauvery in a rowboat, moving along the small islands and watching the crocodiles and the large flocks of birds that fish in the river and nest on the islands.

The Ranganathittu Bird Sanctuary on the river Cauvery is just on the outskirts of Mysore and near to the town of Srirangapatna. There were islets on the river here, which were breeding grounds for a large variety of birds. The sanctuary was also home to many marsh crocodiles.

It was a happy trip; we enjoyed the boat ride, watching the large flocks of birds and their nests. There were the colorful painted storks, the flashing kingfishers, egrets and curlews, pelicans and spoonbills, Terns. The sky and the river were full of birds wheeling, diving, and gliding past. On rocks and edge of the islets there were the crocodiles, sunbathing, motionless. The highlight were two baby crocodiles, but the girls were not enamored of even the tiny crocodiles. The baby crocodiles reminded them of big house lizards.

Later, we had a walk through the extensive gardens. "This is a beautiful place. I expected nothing so lovely," said Sneha.

Veena moved up close to me. "Sorry Krish, I did not mean to hurt you she whispered."

I smiled back at her. "Don't worry Veena, I have taken no offense. What are friends for but to pull each other's legs?"

"So, when are you going to take me for a ride on you bike?" She asked. "Any time I said."

She smiled back at me and moved away, and soon we had reached our parked vehicles. "Why don't you take Bhavna on the bike and come to the restaurant Prasanna" I will drive the car.

Prasanna looked at me, and I could sense his happiness. He looked at Bhavna, who was looking down and blushing a little, but she accepted the helmet I proffered.

"Hey this is not fair," wailed Veena in mock anger, "I was in line for a ride on the bike."

"Yeah, but with me," I laughingly told her.

Veena looked at me, mischief in her eyes. "Promise?" she asked.

"Yes, I promise," I said.

"OK, tomorrow you will pick me up at the Gokulam bus stop at 8.30 am sharp and drop me at my college on your bike," she laughed.

"But what about Bhavna?" I asked. "Oh, she will go with Prasanna as he normally picks us up."

This was news to me. I never knew Prasanna was so involved with them, and he grinned sheepishly at me.

We soon reached the Barge restaurant, which was on the ring road behind the Indian Oil Petrol Pump there.

Sneha looked with interest at the restaurant and mini brewery, which was made totally out of used shipping containers. There was a marvelous use of these old containers and the space available. The containers were old ones meant to be scrapped.

"I really would like to meet the person who designed this," she told us.

Prasanna nodded, silently. He knew the owner of the place.

We enjoyed the food and, as had now become the practice among us, split the bill.

Chapter five

The next day, as promised, I picked up Veena from the Gokulam bus stop. She took her time, slowly walking towards me, preening herself. She was dressed simply in the regulation salwar suit, as the college did not like their students in jeans or such dresses.

I watched her as she walked towards me. She was a petite girl who looked delicate, her large eyes and a cheerful disposition attracted people to her, she was quite pretty too. I liked her, but was wary of her tongue. She could say anything anywhere and was adept at puncturing any swelled-up ego fast.

She reached me and raised her eyebrows. "Have you looked enough or you want to stare some more" she asked giggling. "There is a smudge on your nose," I said straight faced.

She checked in the mirror and then saw me grinning. "Wait, I will get you," she responded.

She sat behind me and we moved off. As we neared the college, she suddenly held me tight, burying her face in my back. I thought she might be hiding from someone; how wrong I was.

There was a large crowd of students near the gate, most of them girls. Veena slowly released me and removed her helmet, handed it over and kissed her fingers to blow me a kiss! I was flabbergasted and embarrassed and quickly left the place and went to our office.

The people in the office seemed to find joy in my presence today. Everyone I passed had a chuckle, and I wondered why.

I popped into Raghu's cabin to let him know I was back and turned to go. "Who is she" asked Raghu. I turned back to him puzzled, he looked at my face and grinned. "Who has marked you out as her territory" he laughed. On my still puzzled look, "go home to change your shirt and come back. Don't let Amma or Appa see you till you change," he said with a laugh.

Puzzled, I went home, removed my shirt and saw that there were lipstick marks on the back! Veena had put them there on purpose, I knew, just for laughs.

Back at the office, Raghu was sitting, looking pensive, when I went inside his office. Seeing me, he shook his head as if to clear something and, smiling, said, "Krish, the architects are coming to discuss and complete the plan. I want you in at the meeting. As of now, the plan seems OK, but you also go through the same and if you wish, you can suggest changes."

The meeting went well; I suggested the only change that we should automate the building to the maximum possible now and also go for multi-layer parking as the number of vehicles was bound to increase. I also suggested that in the Truck parking area we should provide a cafeteria and facilities to our drivers to stay for a day or two if required. This would help us retain drivers who were crucial to our business. Both were well received, and they promised us the final plan by the next day.

Raghu was silent throughout the meeting, which was unusual for him. Sneha was there as the lead architect and she too was silent, letting Govind and Bhaskar, their senior partner, do the discussions. Her only comment was to make a request for a joint visit to the actual location so that they could check the placement of the structures once more.

I expected Raghu to go with them as he was very hands on with the project, but he asked me to go. There was surprise on all faces. I was the junior most person and here was being handed such a responsibility.

Raghu looked at all of them and smiled. "Krish has my complete confidence. He is brilliant and takes his responsibility seriously. From today, he is in complete charge of this project."

It left me stunned; there were claps and congratulations all around. Sneha seemed a bit lost and Govind and Bhaskar were happy as they felt I would be an easier person to deal with. I was diplomatic in speech, whereas Raghu spoke his mind forcefully.

We prepared to go to the site, but as I turned to go, Raghu stopped me. "We need to speak for a minute."

He hugged me as soon as the others left. I was a bit surprised; he was not normally so affectionate in office.

"I am proud of you, Krish. Your suggestions were excellent. I am happy you are taking so much interest in the job. I know you did not wish it and your interests were elsewhere, but be patient and you will soon run this company. Come back and we will discuss. I have big plans for you boy and take the car and driver. I don't want you to ride that dangerous antique bike of yours all around. Let us select a car of your choice today."

I went out bemused and found the others waiting for me. Our driver, Bharat, was waiting by the office vehicle, a Mahindra Scorpio SUV.

We reached the site and went over the details; Sneha was silent mostly. When we were alone, she looked at me and said "you never told me you were Raghu's brother, and I called him fat! Hope you did not tell him that"

I grinned. "I did, and all he said was he needs to play his badminton regularly."

She said nothing to that, but the slightly worried look went from her face. She might have thought the client would be upset.

She went home after I dropped her back at her office. I was happy but my thoughts were a muddled. All the time, I was thinking of Sneha.

Chapter six

The week sped by fast and I kept busy and, on my toes, the project seemed to take a life of its own. Sneha was a person driven to excel, and she seemed very focused on this project. She met with the contractors, discussed the specifications, and was very clear about what she expected from them. She, like Raghu, never minced words.

Raghu kept away from the project completely. He was now focused on getting a business tie up with UltraTech Cement plant at Sedam, a small town near Gulbarga.

Friday morning, he had called a meeting of the other investors and partners of the firm. He held the majority share, but there were a few more partners who had provided part of the capital. He had also asked me to involve the office staff, but he did not specify the agenda.

When the meeting started, it surprised me to see that the heads of our offices in Bangalore, Chennai, Delhi, Kolkata and Mumbai were also there. I also saw that there was a chair next to his at the head of the table. As I moved off to make some arrangement, he called me "Krish, come here, leave the arrangements for someone else". He indicated the chair next to him.

I was surprised, but thought he wanted me to take notes and let him have any information he wanted.

As I sat down, the other partners smiled and nodded at me. There were three of them, all close friends of Raghu.

Raghu began the proceedings as he usually did, straight to the point. "I have called all of you here to let you know we are expanding. I have the cement business tied up and will need to travel frequently to set it up as it is extensive business spread all over India."

He let the clapping and the congratulations stop. "You all know that I have some other big plans, like getting into the LPG transport business as well. These activities will take up a lot of my time and I cannot focus on the day-to-day business, which also needs close attention, especially now that we are building and will shortly move into our new office premises."

He looked around, and I wondered who would be tasked with these responsibilities.

"I have consulted with my other board members and we have unanimously decided to induct Mr. Krishnan Haridasan to the board and appoint him as the Joint Managing Director. All of you will report to him and he will report to me," Raghu announced.

I was stunned; I gazed up at him in surprise. There was a fear in my heart and excitement too.

As the clapping stopped, Raghu looked at me, grinned and said, "so you have nothing to say, you need to give a speech graciously accepting the post," and the others laughed.

I stammered a thank you, as they overwhelmed me with congratulations.

"We will have a celebration of the new business and Krish's promotion tonight. I want all of you there. Let us forget business and have fun today." announced Raghu. "The place is the Country Inn hotel; I have just sent you the invitation with all details today. Come with your families."

He turned to me. "I have already invited our local clients, our vendors, and Prasanna. Invite any other friends you want to." That was Raghu all over, a hard taskmaster but a very generous person, too.

My mobile had been buzzing since long and I found it full of congratulatory messages.

It was a heady feeling to be cherished by your family and praised by your friends.

Chapter seven

The party was a success. Raghu had called the who's who of Mysore. It was the moment that announced that he had arrived. He was now one of the big names in Mysore. But in his typically generous nature, he made the party a moment of my success.

I had invited no one except for Bhavna and Veena, as Raghu had already invited my other friends.

The initial portion of the evening was a daze of introductions and greeting people, a majority of them whom I was meeting for the first time. I realized then that Raghu had set it up so that the people who dealt with us in the business got to know me and I could also know them.

My mom and dad were there, my mother very proud of her two sons and my father looking distinguished in a suit. I had normally seen my father only in his usual dhoti and kurta; seeing him all dressed up showed me what a distinguished-looking man he was. He was friendly with everyone and many went to greet him. It surprised me to see many of the business leaders and politicians go up to him and greet him.

Raghu stood next to me. "It surprised you that father knows so many people and that they are so happy to see him."

I turned to him, and he smiled and spoke

"Father had cleared the IIM entrance exams, but he had no interest in anything but in agriculture. Grandfather let him have his way and gave him some capital with which he bought a small portion of land and then he built on that with his hard work and intelligence and built up the estate that you see now. He also helped all these people, some with money, some with advice, always being there for anyone who came to him."

I was surprised. "I did not know" I said.

"I too got my initial funding from him and the others also came in as they trusted him," said Raghu "Anywhere you go in Mysore or adjacent districts his name opens many doors, remember Krish goodness always pays, whatever good you do, it comes back to you."

He moved off to greet someone, and Govind, who was sitting with Prasanna, Bhavna Veena and Sneha at a table, hailed me.

Prasanna was sipping his normal lime soda, and the girls were having Breezers, a readymade cocktail of fruit-flavored vodka. Govind was sticking to beer today, and I called for a screwdriver, a cocktail of orange juice and vodka. Sneha raised her eyebrows at me and mouthed congratulations. Prasanna smiled and hugged me while the others were more exuberant. Veena held me so tight that I could scarcely breathe. I checked later to see if she had left lipstick marks on my shirt, and she grinned.

Prasanna's boss was there, sitting with Bhaskar and a few of the senior members at a table and explaining something seriously to them. I went to greet them and found the matter under discussion was cocktails made from Rum and how to make them. I had been thinking that they would discuss some complicated business dealing, well I had much to learn.

Prasanna and I were standing alone sometime later. "Strange Raghu and Sneha seem to avoid each other," he said. I glanced at him in surprise and was about to ask him why he thought so. But there was a master of ceremonies and they pulled me into the festivities and action on the stage and forgot all about it.

The evening was a success, and I went home a tired man. I had to go to the office tomorrow and also visit the site.

Chapter eight

Monday brought another surprise, a new cabin next to Raghu's cabin. How had he managed it over just the weekend was a miracle. On the door was my name in gleaming gold letters.

Raghu ushered me in to my cabin with pride.

Raghu felt genuine pride in me, and his gesture moved me. I hugged him and thanked him.

The week passed quickly with meetings with vendors, attending to clients, managing the finances and the cash flow and a thousand other things that went into the day-to-day management of a company.

There were also site visits to check on the progress of the work, following up on clearances with the authorities. Sneha was with me when I visited the site and a big help there; she had become a good friend and though elder to me by a couple of years, I never felt the gap. With Govind, we formed a trio at the site and the informal banter between us eased a lot of pressure on me.

She had stopped calling me a child but still treated me sometimes as a kid and did not hesitate to tell me if she found any of my suggestions stupid. She also had a comment about my lack of dress sense whenever we met, much to the amusement of Govind. I told her that was strange coming from someone who seemed to live always in jeans and kurta.

The clearances from the local authorities were a problem, as I had never dealt with them before. I was wondering whether I would have to involve Raghu. I shared my problem with Sneha and Govind; they laughed at me.

"Have you not discussed this with," Sneha asked.

"Prasanna, why? No, I haven't," I said.

"Don't you know where he works? They have a lot of contacts with the Government authorities and they do a lot of Corporate Social Responsibility work in and around Mysore," said Sneha.

"Prasanna coordinates all this work in Mysore and they keep asking him for setting up toilets in Government schools, solar lights, ambulance and what not," said Govind.

"Every other month there is a photograph of Prasanna with the Collector or the Police Commissioner or the Municipal Commissioner and even photos with the Member of Parliament occasionally," continued Govind.

Well, this was news to me and it went to show how much I was tied up in my own affairs. Prasanna had just joined a few months back in Mysore and already he knew so many people, or rather, so many people knew him. He was a quiet person, but someone you could depend on.

That evening I called Prasanna and explained my problem and he took the details down and promised me action on it immediately. In return, he wanted me to come with him to Srirangapatna on Saturday as he was taking Bhavna and Veena and needed my support. I was surprised and also wondered how he got to know them. I came to know the two girls through Prasanna and normally it was the other way around. Then I remembered Govind, he made friends easily, maybe he had introduced them. But Prasanna seemed to be a bit more involved. He normally avoided girls, thinking them a distraction to his single-minded focus on building his career. I shrugged off the doubts, but I was reluctant knowing Veena would lose no opportunity to tease me. I then invited Sneha to join us and she agreed.

Saturday morning saw all of us gathered at the Nalpak restaurant at VV Mohalla for breakfast as it was near to where Prasanna and the girls stayed. Sneha, too, stayed nearby at an apartment at Jaylakshmipuram.

After a hearty breakfast of Idlis, Vadas and Kesari baath, we set off in my Scorpio, as it would accommodate all of us to the historic town of Srirangapatna.

Srirangapatna was an old town, a power center since ancient times. The Vijayanagara Empire placed its governors in Srirangapatna and controlled the vassal kingdoms of Mysore and Talakad from here.

When the Wodeyars broke away and became independent, they first defeated the Rangaraya, the Vijayanagara Governor at Srirangapatna and controlled the fort of Srirangapatna.

It was the fortified place nearest to Mysore and the last bastion of the rulers of Mysore.

Later, when Hyder Ali took over the kingdom of Mysore, Srirangapatna became his and his son Tipu Sultan's capital.

When the British and the Nizam of Hyderabad defeated and killed Tipu in the fourth Anglo Mysore war in 1799, the Kingdom reverted to the Wodeyars and Srirangapatna lost its importance and Mysore city gained in prominence as it was the seat of the Wodeyars, the rulers of Mysore since the 12th Century.

I was explaining all this to Sneha, Bhavna and Veena. Govind was dozing off while Prasanna focused on driving. Whenever we went anywhere, it was Prasanna, or me, who drove as both of us loved driving.

"Everyone knows Srirangapatna only in connection with Tipu or because of the Brindavan gardens," I said. "But it is an ancient settlement and there are many ancient and beautiful places in and around the town."

"The temple of Ranganatha swamy is itself ancient and is a revered place of worship. But for me, the Temple of Chennakesava, at Somnath Pura, is the favorite because of its amazing architecture." I went on.

Govind looked up at me wryly and went back to his napping with a sigh and Prasanna laughed.

Sneha asked "can we see the temple of Chennakesava also then" Prasanna nodded as Govind sighed again.

We spent the morning in praying at the ancient temple of Ranganatha swamy. We then moved to the places associated with Tipu, especially where he was supposed to have fallen fighting to the last breath.

The girls read the plaque erected at the memorial with interest.

Tipu was a brave man and a great general. Sadly, he had now become a figure of controversy

He had fought the British to a standstill, modernized the Mysore army, improved administrative practices, and the kingdom of Mysore prospered under him. He was one of the best rulers of his time. But he was also a harsh man who brooked no opposition and could be ruthless to achieve his own ends.

To the Kodava people of Coorg, he was a betrayer and a murderer who committed genocide on them.

The Melkote Iyengars remembered him as a ruler who killed innocents, including women and children, the night before Diwali.

For the Nairs of Kerala, he was a barbarian enemy who dishonored even the dead and tried to exterminate them.

To the Mangalorean Christians, he was the one who nearly exterminated them.

I explained the enigma that Tipu was and how misunderstood both sides were about him

Govind and Prasanna knew my views of Tipu and remained silent. The girls moved away at last and we went to the Karnataka Tourism resort for lunch.

The resort by the banks of the Cauvery was a favorite place of mine. You could sit on the banks of the river and watch it play as it flowed forcefully. You could also take a Coracle ride is the rushing waters and enjoy the thrill of the fast-flowing river up close.

It was pleasant sitting on the steps, sipping beer and watching the river flow in all its majesty.

But Veena was having none of that. I believe she liked to disturb my serenity. She jumped up and went to the lone coracle operator there, negotiated with him, and soon I found myself in a spinning coracle.

Both Bhavna and Veena screamed in fear, but they seemed to enjoy it. I could see Bhavna reach out and hold Prasanna's hand. He held it and smiled reassuringly at her. Veena immediately caught hold of my hand. I tried to get, but she held it tighter.

We reached the middle of the river, now only a little distance from the shore, but as the coracle was low in the water and the river rushed by, it felt terrifying to people unaccustomed to it. I was accustomed to coracle rides and knew what was coming next. The boatman, with a few expert thrusts of the oar, made the coracle spin around fast in the water. To people unaccustomed to this, it was very frightening and dizzying. Bhavna and Veena stopped their screaming. Veena held my hand tighter and buried her face in my shoulder. I could feel Sneha clutch my other arm. Prasanna had enough of seeing the girls frightened. He snarled at the boatman "stop you idiot" who looked surprised and affronted at the same time. One look at Prasanna's face and he stopped the spinning.

The girls soon recovered from their fright and enjoyed the rather placid return, with Prasanna continuing to hold Bhavna's hand. Sneha had let go of me, but Veena seemed to find solace in holding my hand and keeping her head on my shoulder. I squirmed and tried to break free, but she would not let go.

We then proceeded to the Temple of Chennakesava at Somnath Pura.

This was an ancient temple built during the period of the Hoysala Empire.

Somnatha Dandanayaka, a commander of the Hoysala Empire, built this and other temples in the area.

The wars of the period between the Deccan sultanates and the other kingdoms saw many of those temples destroyed.

Here also there are signs of the destruction wrought and there is no regular worship here. Chennakesava means handsome Keshava, and this is truly a beautiful temple dedicated to that handsome god.

The main temple with its symmetrical beauty and the well laid out gardens under an azure sky was picture perfect when we reached the place.

Everyone was silent as they took in the place's beauty. I had timed it so that the crowds would be less because everyone would rush off to the Brindavan gardens to see the musical fountains and lighting.

Sneha was silent taking in the place, she turned to me and said "Thank you Krish, this is really a marvelous place."

We had an excellent time, or rather, I had. Ancient structures always enamored me. This was a gem of a temple and found it very pleasant to explain it to three pretty ladies.

Sneha asked a lot of questions, and I surprised myself by answering most of them. She looked at me, smiled and said "well you really are passionate about this temple, your city, and when you also get involved and forget to be shy," even as I puffed up at this praise, "It is good to see kids even today interested in such things."

Kid! She had called me a kid! I reddened, and Veena giggled and whispered Kuzhanthai at me.

I mumbled something and moved away to sit under the enormous tree, which spread shade and solace to suffering souls.

Prasanna had been talking to someone for some time on the phone and soon hustled us into the car.

"I have a surprise for you," he said and refused to say anymore.

We soon were at the Brindavan dam, and Prasanna drove right towards the top of the dam. I was surprised; the area was a prohibited place for the last few years and you could not go on top of the dam.

The security at the gate stopped us. Prasanna flashed his company ID. The policeman noted the vehicle number and opened the gate and waved us through. He only told us to come back the same way as the other gate was locked.

Prasanna smiled. "Our dealer nearby supplies the fuel to the police station under whose jurisdiction this area falls. I asked him to make a request," was all the explanation he would offer.

The water level was high, and we parked the car and walked on top of the dam. We could see the massive sluice gates which were closed now, but still some water was squeezing through as a spray.

It was pleasant walking there on the top, peaceful with no crowds, birds wheeling about, the gentle movement of the water lapping the shores and the dam.

After this, no one really wanted to see the dancing fountains in the garden below. It seemed very banal after what we felt on the top of the dam.

The lights were coming on and soon it would be dark and we called it a day after dinner.

We reached Frosting at Vani Vilas, or VV Mohalla, as we locals called it. This was a restaurant in an old graceful bungalow which had an eclectic menu, a bit of continental, a bit of Italian. Some Indian fusion was the food on offer. I quite liked it, though both Prasanna and Govind had more plebeian tastes, in my opinion.

I was sure the girls would love it and Govind and Prasanna had agreed a bit reluctantly.

The food came along with the mock tails we had ordered. Sneha looked around. "nice" she said.

I beamed and replied, "Great, I knew you would like the food. These two guys here wanted to go to the Purohit and have samosas."

"Oh, I meant the ambiance they have created and how well they have used the space," Sneha replied "The mock tails are good and I guess the food is nice though a little bland, I love samosas and Indian food, give me a good Vada pav any day, hot and spicy,"

"Me too," chimed in the others. There was a smile on the plebeian face of my friends as I mumbled and stumbled to reply.

"Don't worry, I am sure you meant well," said Sneha, patting me on the back. Govind choked as Veena patted me on the head and said "Kuzhanthai, check with everyone next time".

I shrugged, and we called it a day going off to our respective homes.

Chapter nine

The days fled past with work and more work. Raghu was flying off to Delhi and Mumbai almost every other day.

Our fleet was expanding and the work at our new complex proceeded fast. Prasanna had delivered on his promise of a quick clearance.

Sneha and me were often together, not just at work, but often we caught a quick lunch or a snack at the many small eateries at Gokulam.

There was no time for any trips, though we vaguely discussed going to the Bandipur Tiger sanctuary.

I was restless. There was so much going on at the work front, but my personal life was empty. I felt unfulfilled.

I did not know what was happening. There was the pressure of work, but I normally thrived on pressure.

Raghu now left most of the day-to-day work for me. He was busy tying up a big contract and was planning a foray into cement transportation. He had friends in Namakkal, the hub of the transport business in South India. Many of them were second or third generation in the transport business. They were young, well-educated and widely traveled. Their fathers and grandfathers had started with little capital and many had started as drivers who then became owners and expanded.

The youngsters were changing how the transport industry operated. They were smart, tech savvy, willing to innovate and to take risks. Raghu was part of this young group. They supported each other and there was a unity among them which helped them negotiate better deals with their customers and the suppliers, especially the petroleum companies.

My own dreams were of an Azure Sea under a blue sky and I felt trapped now. I coped as I normally did in any situation, but felt ill-used that they had not even consulted me before making me shoulder so much responsibility. Most people in my situation would have been happy to be in my position and grateful to have a brother like Raghu. But something inside me wanted more, an opportunity to prove myself.

I had few friends with whom I would be comfortable in opening up. Prasanna was my closest friend, and he was not available. Prasanna was busy with his own work. One officer from his department had left, and he had additional burdens and could spare little time and many weekends also he was traveling.

Govind was just a friend.

WE MET ON SATURDAY evenings, me, Govind, Sneha, Bhavna and Veena. Prasanna joined us when he could. I could sense Bhavna's frustration when he did not come. Veena often pulled my leg when we met and I found it released my unhappiness to some extent as I laughed at her witticisms at my expense.

One Saturday as I laughed at Veena's imitation of my serious demeanor as I contemplated the menu and instructed the waiter on how I wanted the Kabab prepared, Veena stopped and said "You know Krish you are such a sweet person and a sport, I have watched you these last few weeks and the pressure you are under and yet you don't get upset when I tease you"

"Yes," said Sneha, "Krish is a really sweet person, very understanding, helpful and patient."

Prasanna, who had joined us that day, raised his eyebrows at me and smiled. I squirmed, embarrassed.

The moment passed, but I felt happy that my friends were there. I looked at Sneha and Veena affectionately, smiling. They smiled back and Veena patted my hand, "don't let it swell your head, Kuzhanthai" she said, bringing me down to earth.

The work was taking a toll on me and I became impatient with people. I was normally the patient guy in the office, but with Raghu increasingly leaving the day-to-day workings to me fully, I was worried I might make a mistake.

Sneha and Govind were with me the day I lost my temper fully with the contractor working on our site. He had been promising more speed and was not delivering on the same, and my frustration boiled over.

Rayappa, the contractor, was a much older person, with an excellent reputation and a friend of my father. He was deeply hurt and humiliated at my shouting at him in public.

Govind looked at me in surprise and tried to calm me down and finally I stopped. Sneha too was surprised, "Take it easy Krish, there is a problem in getting good labor and we are within schedule" she said.

I mumbled an apology to everyone and left with no further word. I knew what I was doing was wrong, but my anger had hold of me and if I stayed back, I would make it worse.

Evening when I came home my mother was hovering around waiting for me. "Rayappa is here talking with your father," she said. "How could you do this, Krishna? You are such a sweet boy and Rayappa is not just any vendor. He is like a brother to me and an uncle to you."

I went to my room without replying. Half an hour later, my father called me.

"Krish, I think you need a break; you have been working too hard. In fact, both of you boys are working too hard, and I insist we take a few days off."

"Appa, I am sorry about what happened with Rayappa," I began. My father cut me off. "That is not an issue. As a contractor, if he has not kept his word, he deserves what he got. I told him and your mother both the same. Our relationship is outside our work. If you were to shout at him inside this house, I would take you to task," said my father.

I was surprised, and he smiled back at me. "It is his own fault; I had told him initially not to take the work and even if he takes it, his son should supervise it. He is lucky it is you dealing with him. Raghu would have shouted at him so many times by now," my father laughed.

"From tomorrow his son will take over, so don't worry too much," said my father.

"But I am worried about you. You are such a balanced person, losing your temper is not expected."

My father explained. "Are you still moping about not doing what you wanted to do and joining Raghu?" asked my father.

"No Appa, am fine, just tired with the work and worried as it is all new to me."

"Be ready this Friday evening. We are all going to a home stay in Kodagu. I have booked the whole home stay and have also invited Prasanna and Govind, plan with them and be ready to leave by four pm," ordered my father.

Raghu came in late that night and made no objections to the program. "Yes, we need a break, but I would have given a lot to see you lose your temper, kid," he grinned. "You are always so well behaved and disciplined."

I mumbled an embarrassed reply and moved off to sleep.

Chapter ten

Prasanna called me on Friday morning to fix up where we would meet. He would pick up the girls and Govind. I was surprised; I did not know the girls were also coming, but he said my father had called each one of them personally and told them to come.

Raghu, when he heard the girls were coming, said nothing. During lunch, he told us he had to leave for Mumbai and could not join us. I was disappointed; I enjoyed vacations with Raghu; he was fun and totally unpredictable on vacations. I had missed that fun loving Raghu for some years now.

My father said nothing then but while getting up from lunch he looked at Raghu and said "No son of mine is a coward, see that you are here at 3.30 pm, we leave at 4 pm" Raghu looked at my mother entreatingly "I agree, for once, with Hari, be here by 3.30 pm," said my mother.

Raghu had no choice. He shrugged and nodded. My father was easygoing most of the time, but once that tone came in his voice, we all knew it was better not to argue with him.

The evening saw us all meet at the petrol pump which Prasanna had asked us to come to. We were in our Scorpio SUV, the four of us, while Prasanna was in his Honda Amaze. Raghu was driving, and we fueled at the pump.

It was funny watching the petrol pump guys who usually would not bother about customers suddenly become super responsive on seeing Prasanna. They cleaned our wind shield asked us if we needed our tire pressure checked. They were all greeting us with a Namaste and asking us to check the zero on the dispenser before they fueled.

I grinned at Govind and we looked towards Prasanna, who was watching everything keenly and not saying a word. The pump owner was standing next to him, looking anxious.

It always surprised both Govind and me at the reaction Prasanna got at their company pumps. He was a soft-spoken, polite young man, and we wondered why the pump staff and owners were so worried when he stepped into their pumps.

We left, and I took the wheel and we were soon on the road speeding towards Bylakuppe, our first halt.

We took a break at Bylakuppe at the Tibetan Cooperative run petrol pump as it had well maintained public toilets which the ladies could use.

The girls looked at the Tibetan staff in curiosity. Bhavna stiffened as the lady manager, a beautiful Tibetan girl, came out and greeted Prasanna. They offered us momos and Tibetan Tea which we politely refused.

My father than suggested that he would drive the Honda Amaze as he wanted to spend time with Amma, Prasanna and the others could shift to the Scorpio so that we youngsters could be together.

We were all enthusiastic, but Raghu was reluctant. "What will I do with the kids, and it is difficult to drive as the light fades and the road climbs and twist," he told my father.

My father smilingly said "Son I have been driving on these roads in much worse conditions much before you were born, now let me spent time with my wife with no distractions from you kids, and yes Raghu you are also a kid don't forget."

Raghu seemed reluctant, but could not prevail over my father. I handed over the keys to him, but he refused. "I will sit at the back with Govind," he said

"No anna, I will sit at the back with Bhavna as we are smaller. Let Veena sit with Krish in the front seat, as she is prone to travel sickness in the middle seat. Sneha, you and Govind can be comfortable in the middle seat," said Prasanna.

I was bemused I could understand Prasanna wanting to be with Bhavna, but why should Veena come to the front? Travel sickness, I could not believe it. This was a girl who had traveled on the roof of the bus on one of our trips. But I kept my mouth shut, as Prasanna usually had good reasons for whatever he did.

My brother looked grim as he entered the Scorpio. Govind, at the last minute, had claimed the window seat and Raghu would have to sit between Sneha and Govind. I thought I understood his reluctance. It would be cramped there.

The home stay we had booked was inside a plantation a little ahead of Somwarpet in Kodagu district. Prasanna often stayed there and knew the owners and the staff.

I drove with my attention focused on the road and did not really pay much attention to the back. But after some time felt that the silence was oppressive. Raghu would normally crack jokes or tell us about the places we crossed and Sneha would keep asking questions when we traveled. But today both were silent.

Veena, who normally would chatter away and pull my leg, was also silent. I could sense that Raghu was unhappy and now felt that Sneha, too, seemed a bit off in her mood. I was wondering what could I do.

Govind came to the rescue. "Why don't you put on some music and maybe we can sing along?" he said. "Yes, let's do that," said Veena and Bhavna.

Veena immediately took the phone from my pocket, leaning against me, much to my embarrassment.

I focused on the road as it became narrower with blind corners and turns as we climbed up into the mountains.

The others sang, and the surprise was Raghu joining in the singing with gusto. Sneha, too, seemed to come to life and joined in. I stayed silent.

Veena hushed every one after sometime "I am going to put on our sweet driver's favorite song and he will sing it along with all of us,"

I demurred, I only sang when I was in the bathroom or when I had a few too many. But Veena was relentless, and the others added their demands.

Harry Belafonte came on the speakers with his Jamaica farewell and I listened to it with pleasure and the tension left me. I was with family and friends driving through some of the most beautiful sections in Karnataka and my happiness burst out in joining in singing the song.

We reached the plantation home stay just before dark and were welcomed with hot coffee and piping hot dal vadas.

The place was beautiful, an oasis set amidst verdant greenery. The accommodation was basic: there were four rooms, two with three beds, one with a double bed and a tiny one with a single bed.

I soon sorted us out, my parents in the double room, Raghu in the single bedroom, the girls in one of the three beds and we boys in the other.

My parents were happy to see me and Raghu laughing and joking. Raghu looked around and sighed. "What a lovely place, kid. We should plan something like this place".

The next couple of days we spent in exploring the nearby places, trekking to a nearby waterfall and bathing in it. My father also showed off his prowess in swimming in the small lake on the estate, beating all of us.

Raghu seemed to come out of his shell. He was the life and soul of the group. Sneha matched him in everything and they seemed to be together most of the time.

We went back on Sunday night, a tired but happy group.

Chapter eleven

The next few weeks were all hectic, but I remained balanced and in control of my temper. Sneha was often with me as the work of our new premises picked up speed.

It became a practice for us. I would pick her up from her office a little before lunch. We would visit the site and go over the progress and then have lunch together, discussing work or just chatter away.

We grew close to each other; I shared my dreams of being a Naval officer and sailing around the world. She remained silent about her own dreams.

I found her easy to talk to and loved watching her. When she caught me staring at her, there would be a frown on her face and she would glare. I would smile and she would shake her head and move away.

She seemed to withdraw a little after she caught me staring at her. I became careful to avoid giving her any offence and controlled myself and we became normal again.

If I did not see her even once in a day, I felt restless and made some excuse to see her. I agreed with her on most things, and I attempted to keep her happy. I realized one day that she occupied too much of my thoughts. Was this love? I wondered.

She was a lovely woman, independent, apt to speak her mind and seemed comfortable around me.

On weekends, we visited many of the nearby places along with Govind, Prasanna, Veena and Bhavna.

A couple of weeks later, Raghu asked me if I had visited Kabini recently. He was considering a property there. We could go early morning on Saturday, check out the property and have some fun. "Ask your friends too. I have already invited Sneha," he said. I was surprised but thought little about it.

We saw the property and did not like it. But otherwise, the day was fun. We went for the safari and saw an elusive leopard.

Raghu was at his charming best and seemed very happy. He had just bought a new Mahindra Thar that he planned to do off roading in. He asked Sneha to go with him for a ride in it the next day.

I was surprised and jealous when she accepted. Raghu normally took me on such ventures, and this was the first time he had not asked me.

I was about to protest when Prasanna nudged me to keep quiet.

The next week, everything seemed normal. Sneha met me as usual and we had lunch together.

But the weekend brought changes. I had planned a trip to Melkote and its temples, but Sneha excused herself.

I went with the others, but the day seemed drab and dull to me.

The next week, there was a change. Raghu joined me and Sneha on many days and we three had lunch together. My mother was not happy. Both her sons were not having lunch in the house now.

On weekends now, Raghu too joined us whenever he was in Mysore and seemed to monopolize Sneha.

The work at the office was proceeding at a fast pace. Sneha delegated to Govind much of the work as she became busy with another project. Her visits to the site were less frequent now.

I watched the developments with anxiety; I knew now that I loved Sneha, but I loved my brother, too. Sneha stopped coming with us when Raghu was not there and he was rarely around, as he was busy with setting up the new division. Whenever he was in town, he would join us and Sneha would come too. They never seemed to go alone together anywhere, but we could see the spark between them.

I did not know what to do. If it was someone else, I would have been jealous and tried my best to woo Sneha.

But being jealous of Raghu made me feel ashamed. I still hoped that what they had was friendship.

Chapter twelve

It was a new emotion for me, this yearning, the anger and the heartache. There was guilt because I loved my brother.

I became careless of my appearance, often reporting to the office unshaven and in casual clothes. I was no longer attentive or sharp as before. My focus was lost. The work got done as routine kicked in and systems took care of any slack. My team was dedicated and required little supervision.

I skipped lunch to avoid seeing Sneha and Raghu together. I grabbed a sandwich or subsisted on tea or coffee. I skipped the weekend trips and mumbled some excuse or the other.

Prasanna watched me with concern, and my mother nagged me to eat. My father was silent, but I could see the concern in his eyes. Raghu was too busy with his work and Sneha to notice anything amiss.

Everyone thought it was the work and the need to prove myself that was taking its toll on me.

I disliked to be among people and took to going away on my bike in the evenings with a couple of bottles of beers. I usually rode up to the Chamundi hills and found a secluded place, sitting there, sipping beer, my mind a blank. The sun went down. As the lights went up in Mysore as I sat in the darkness above. The darkness in me seemed to find solace in being alone and watching the lights far below.

It was now two months since I fell into a routine, avoiding my friends and family, being stoic and uncommunicative. It gave me pleasure to watch the worried looks on the faces of those close to me.

Bitterness rose like bile inside, but I kept a tight lid and hugged my misery to myself.

I was oblivious to the misery I was causing wrapped up as I was in my world of self-pity. It needed a shock to jolt me out.

I was on the hilltop one weekend with my bottles of beer, watching the lights come up as the light faded away. I sighed, stretched and got on my bike and rode down the hills, taking the familiar curves without being my normal alert self. Round one corner there was a temporary police check post set up to check drunken driving. I got caught.

I sat in the darkness on the milestone, jolted out of my apathy by the harsh tones of the policeman. He looked at me with contempt. "Rich kid wasting father's money and endangering others," he said as he waved me off to the side to await my turn in the proceedings.

I could not call on my family. It would mortify them and hurt; their son arrested for drunken driving! I called up Prasanna, and he drove up soon with a rider for my bike. He knew the policeman and spoke with him and smoothed ruffled feathers. I paid the fine. My driver's license was returned with an admonition from the policeman to avoid such behavior in the future.

I got into the car, expecting Prasanna to lecture and shout at me. I sighed and waited for his tirade. I should have known my friend better. He just smiled. "How do you feel? Why don't you freshen up and join us for dinner?"

He smiled wryly at my surprise. "Krish, you are a balanced person with high intelligence. You know, your behavior was illogical. I don't need to point that out to you."

I was silent; I was lucky to have a friend like this; I knew I did not have to thank him; he understood my feelings.

I agreed to dinner, and he took me to my house to change and get ready. As I was getting down, he stopped me, he looked at me in the eyes and said, "look at yourself in the mirror and see what you have done to yourself." He was silent for a few seconds and then said softly, "let her go Krish."

I gaped at him. He nodded and gave a faint smile and drove off.

I showered and stood in front of the mirror. There were bags under my eyes, my beard was straggly and my mustache was untrimmed. My finger nails had grown and my hair was straggly and unkept. I had lost weight and my once muscled body was a shadow of itself. I could not believe I had gone downhill so fast.

Prasanna picked me up shortly and thankfully Sneha and Raghu were not joining us that day. Bhavna and Veena looked at me as if at a stranger. We were meeting after a long time. They both hugged me and Veena held me tight for a long time. I sighed. She was up to her old tricks, but when she left me, I could see the glint of tears in her eyes. Bhavna, too, looked at me with concern. Veena kept patting my hand as she sat next to me. I was touched; I did not deserve friends like this. Dinner was a rather sedate affair with Veena, not teasing me as usual and the others being careful in what they said.

I put my fork down and glared at Veena in mock anger, "why are you behaving so prim and proper, no teasing or leg pulling today? Are you not well or you think I can no longer bear it?" I asked her.

There was a chuckle at that from her "Kuzhanthai, good to see you try to grow up" said Veena, but there was more of a caress in her voice than mockery which I did not understand then.

Prasanna and Bhavna smiled at that, and things became normal to a large extent.

I went home that night in a much better frame of mind. I thought about what had happened and understood that I had been selfish and in lolling about in my misery had caused misery to others who did not deserve it. I resolved to do better and slept well that night.

Morning brought a lightness and acceptance in my heart. I shaved and groomed myself carefully and felt the warmth of my mother's smile when she saw me. My father patted me on the back and I could sense his relief and happiness. Raghu was out of town.

In the office too I could sense the change in the atmosphere, people seemed to be more willing to do what I wanted and cheerfully at that.

I was dreading having lunch all alone but need not have bothered. At 1 pm Bhavna and Veena walked into my office with Subway sandwiches, a favorite of mine. Prasanna was out of town on one of his many tours. We sat in my room eating in a silent companionship. The girls looked at me and smiled and Veena patted my clean-shaven face. "Kuzhanthai" she murmured.

I felt a sense of lightness after their visit and set about my work in a much happier frame of mind.

The darkness was still in me, a gnawing pain that refused to go away. I put up a cheerful front and tried to get back to my routine. My friends helped. Always there was Bhavna, Veena and or Prasanna coming around for lunch and dinner. My evening excursions on the bike stopped as I entered society once more. My friends never asked me about the dark phase in my life and they never discussed Sneha. I knew they understood a lot even without me saying anything.

I went for early morning runs and that brought on the loneliness again, but not for long. A few days later, Veena joined me on my run. I was surprised and wondering why she had joined me; she read the question in my eyes and smiled. "I am the champion long-distance runner of my college and regularly go for long runs. It helps me not only remain fit but also cheerful against all odds."

I looked at her afresh and she gazed back at me with those large eyes of hers. She was a small, petite girl and looked delicate. But there was steel in her and appearances could be deceptive. She easily kept up with me and then stepped up the pace and I had to stretch myself to the utmost to keep up with her. As we stopped and I caught my breath, she grinned at me and I grinned back. Yes, running got me to forget my troubles, but I think it was also her cheerfulness that rubbed off on me.

A fortnight went by and I struggled, but kept the darkness at bay. Raghu returned and joined us on a Sunday as we drove to a farm in Mandya for a country lunch of Ragi Mudde, balls of millet which you dipped in gravy and ate, and other local fare.

Sneha was there with him; I was seeing her after a long time and I felt the familiar dull ache rise in my heart.

Prasanna was watching me, and I shrugged and got a grip on myself. The lunch itself was forgettable. I never liked Raagi Mudde.

Chapter thirteen

I could not avoid Sneha and she often come to the office to discuss the interiors of our new building. Raghu left me to decide on the interiors and I was often with Sneha. It was a torture to me to see her so frequently, yet there was happiness and pleasure in her company. She still treated me like a kid and seemed to find nothing amiss in my behavior.

But I avoided going for lunch and avoided her as much as possible. As Veena and Bhavna were often around, it was easy for me to avoid being alone with her.

The date for our new office inauguration was fixed, and the pace picked up. I had no time to dwell on my pain.

The day of the inauguration came, and it seemed our parents had called everyone. Our relatives from all over seemed to be there. I had not seen many of them for years and I seemed to be the cynosure of all my aunts. They all hugged me and expressed surprise over how I had grown. Raghu seemed to avoid getting these attentions as he made sarcastic comments to some of them.

As another aunt enfolded me in a cloying embrace, exclaiming over my growth, I could see Veena grinning at me. There was a mischievous glint in her eyes. I hurried off. There were cousins and uncles and so many people whom I had never seen all coming and chatting me up.

Raghu was with a group of his friends and people his own age and had clarified that this whole thing was my show. Sneha was with him.

I got a tap on my head and turned to find my favorite cousin. Jyoti was nearly my height, and her eyes twinkled at me as I gaped at her. "Jyo," I exclaimed in joy and caught her hands. "When did you return to India? Where are you now?" She was my age, and we had shared many vacations together as children. A few years back she was the talk of the family as she left a well-paying job in Mumbai to go travel around the world on her own.

Jyoti gripped my hands. "It is good to see you too Krish, I am currently in Pondicherry living at Auroville so thought I would come and see all of you. I heard you too were in Pondicherry some time back."

"Yes, I was, and we need to catch up. It is great to see you." I grinned back at her. "Well, some people at least do not think so." She replied wryly, and I turned to find her mother glaring at her. We walked towards her hand in hand. Her mother was my father's elder sister, normally a sweet, laid-back woman.

"Hi Amma," greeted Jyoti and my aunt snorted and spoke. "You know Krish, this girl left us at Chennai and went to Mumbai years back and from there she went God knows where and now instead of coming home to us she meets us here."

"That is because if I come, you start that old tale of how I should get married, and now no one will marry me," retorted Jyoti.

"Hey, I will marry you anytime you want," I said. "No, you are too respectable for me," Jyoti said and laughed; I joined her. My Aunt rolled her eyes at that. I used to follow Jyoti around when I was young and insist that I would marry her only.

We moved away and Jyoti whispered to me, "that is another person who is looking at us with disfavor" I turned and found Veena looking at us with a frown from across the room. "Who is that, your girlfriend?"

"No, just a friend." I replied, "she is probably hungry and as I had promised to have lunch with her and Bhavna, she is waiting for me. Come and join us."

We went together and Veena lost her frown once Jyoti told her about some of our escapades together.

Bhavna and Veena had to leave after lunch as they had a workshop to attend at their college and Prasanna left with them.

"Nice girl, your girlfriend. Tell me about her," said Jyoti. I protested, but she suddenly stiffened, saying, "What is she doing here?"

I turned to see Sneha laughing at something Raghu had said.

Jyoti seemed upset. She got up saying, "God, the guts of that woman coming here."

I followed her out and asked her what was the matter. "I will tell you later dear Krish, anyway it is none of my business if Raghu has accepted her. I am staying the Country Inn, have dinner with me," and she left.

I was mystified, but before I could follow her, my mother pulled me away.

At last, the day ended, and I freshened up, changed into casual clothes and rode my bike to meet Jyoti. I wanted to show her my bike and talk about old times.

I found Jyoti in a perturbed mood; she took me immediately to an isolated table. We ordered a bottle of Dindori Reserve Shiraz wine to go with the buffet dinner.

We made small talk till the wine arrived and Jyoti fell silent after some time. She looked at me with troubled eyes. "How long has that woman been here?" she asked. I shrugged. "A year now. Why do you ask?"

"Don't you know who she is? The woman who nearly destroyed Raghu!" exclaimed Jyoti.

I sat up, and seeing my surprise, she shrugged. "I guess no one told you and you were not here, so you would not know."

This the tale which she told me as we finished the bottle of wine was upsetting but cleared up many things for me.

Raghu had gone to do his MBA from the SP Jain Institute of Management, a reputed educational institute in India.

There he met Sneha, who was from Mumbai and doing her architecture course from the JJ College of Architecture. Her family had roots in Karnataka but had lived for generations in Mumbai. Her father was a reputed businessman in the city, with contacts in administrative and political circles.

They became friends and then fell in love. As they were both straightforward and focused individuals, they decided they would finish their courses and establish themselves before consummating their relationships. They also felt pride in each other and informed their families.

Sneha's parents, especially her father, Shivraj, had strong reservations about their relationship. He did not want his only child to get into a relationship with an unknown boy who was the son of a nondescript farmer from the hinterland of Karnataka. For Mumbaikars, as a typical Mumbai person is called, any town in India outside Mumbai was a hick town. He wanted a scion of a big business family as his son-in-law.

Sneha was adamant and there were frequent quarrels in the house over the issue. Raghu had not informed his parents as he waited for acceptance from Sneha's family. He was confident that his family would happily accept his choice.

But Raghu chafed at the restrictions and took matters into his hands. He spoke to Sneha, and against her wishes, planned to meet her parents.

One evening, Raghu went with Sneha to meet her parents. What transpired there no one knows but Raghu came back furious. Jyoti was much younger than both of them, but had heard the elders talk. Sneha decided she could not face the constant trauma at home and told Raghu to see if he could find a small apartment so that they could live together.

This brought things to a head. Sneha's father called up Raghu and warned him not to meet his daughter anymore. Raghu refused.

Sneha's father used his contacts, and the police picked Raghu up on false charges of eve teasing. They thrashed him badly in custody and Raghu's friends informed my father.

My father came to Mumbai. He had his own contacts in Karnataka, and through them he had Raghu freed and the case quashed. He also met Sneha's father in his office and warned him that any further attacks on his son would lead to very unpleasant circumstances for Shivraj and his family. Sneha's father was shocked to find that someone whom he had dismissed as a country bumpkin was an urbane person with his own contacts. He promised not to do anything further but expressed his unhappiness at the alliance.

My father loved his son and wished to see him happy. He spoke to Sneha and assured her he would welcome her happily and support her. He said that Sneha could leave her parents' house and come to Mysore, and he would get them married.

Sneha had been bold enough to tell Raghu to find a house so that they could live together. But what happened after that had hit her hard and she lost her confidence. It is difficult for a girl to go against her parents. Her ties of love and belonging bind her. Change is also a something we all fear. Sneha, a young girl just out of her teens, then could not gather the courage to leave. My father also, though he promised support, was not in favor or her abandoning her parents.

Sneha stayed with her parents, and Raghu was hurt and angry at her decision. He turned around and left. He never returned her calls or spoke to her after that. Father tried to make him understand, but Raghu was adamant.

Raghu finished his course, came back to Mysore and immersed himself in his work. He never socialized or went out with any woman. He refused all proposals for marriage and became a bit of a recluse.

Now that I knew the background, I was mortified and ashamed to some extent.

I told Jyoti some of what had happened and she seemed mollified. It was clear Sneha had come to Mumbai chasing Raghu.

I could now understand the situation, but accepting it was hard. Every time I saw Sneha it was with a pang, a pain and there was desolation in the horizon.

Chapter fourteen

Life slipped back into a routine. We shifted into our new premises. This brought more challenges for me and I was constantly busy and on my toes. This helped me avoid slipping back into my darkness.

I met Sneha rarely now but Raghu was at Mysore more now. He sent me to many of the meetings outside Mysore and I got to know a lot more about the business and logistics. Raghu had also given me a small share of the business as a bonus for all my hard work.

Raghu seemed under stress. He laughed a lot less and seemed to be lost in thought many a time. I took up the slack in the office, too.

I knew Raghu was meeting Sneha, as I saw them having dinner together at many places. Mysore is a small town and there are limited places where you can go for dinner. Most of the people at these places knew me and Raghu and they would offer to seat us near him.

It was embarrassing and also hurt me to see them together. I gathered courage one day and asked Raghu to tell where he was going so I and my friends could avoid going to that place in evening. For the first time, I saw my brother hesitate, and he looked embarrassed. He gave me a sheepish grin and told me where he was going for dinner that day.

The work piled on and I was always under stress. It was work which I was good at but did not really love. I liked a bit of adventure, travel and, to some extent, I was also a loner. I was sensitive but feared showing or sharing my emotions, so kept my emotions under control and showed a stoic face to the world.

Mysore was a small city and you could not avoid people in the same circle or social milieu for long. I often met Sneha and Raghu having lunch together at the office or together at some event. I could not avoid and had to join them sometimes. These times were difficult for me and took all my resolve not to break.

The work did not help, and I was often silent when I went out with friends. I slept badly and had dark circles under my eyes.

My friends and family assumed it was because of the work pressure, and I kept quiet. Veena often came alone to have lunch with me or just be there for me. Prasanna too either met or called me daily.

One day Prasanna came alone in the evening and insisted that I go with him. We went to one of our favorite spots. High on Chamundi hills with my beautiful city of Mysore spread out below us. The Lalitha Mahal Palace was visible in all its beauty.

Prasanna was a straightforward person and did not beat about the bush. He spoke straight away.

"I am worried about you Krish, no don't protest, we both know why and I will say nothing about it. But you cannot go on like this, it will affect your family. That you are trapped in a job which you don't really enjoy also does not help. You need to think for yourself and decide what you want to do. Give yourself a chance at happiness."

I sighed. "She loves my brother, and he loves her. What can I do?"

Prasanna laughed. "Is that your only love? You have many things to be grateful for. I know you very well Krish, you are a balanced person; do not go around like this. At least it is good you have not started to drink again and are taking care of yourself. There are many other people you love and who love you back and there is your big dream." He held out a newspaper to me.

Surprised, I took the paper and opened it and found Prasanna had marked a notification that had come that day. It was from the Indian Navy about the Indian Navy Entrance Test for graduate level entries. I looked at Prasanna, who smiled. "You meet all the requirements, Krish. Your passion will get you through and you would have taken the first step in your lifelong dream."

I looked at him, and he could see the emotions in my eyes. Being a naval officer was a childhood dream, and it had never left me. It was something I aspired to, but there was fierce opposition from my family. My mother had lost one of her brothers, an army man, in the Kargil war and my father agreed with her. Raghu, too, did not wish to see me go; his dream was for both of us to build a business empire together.

I had no desire to build a business empire. My focus and intelligence would get me through and I had already proven myself in Raghu's business, but it brought me no happiness. I dearly wanted to apply, but my love for my family held me back,

Prasanna understood without me having to speak about my dilemma. He looked at the horizon and sighed. He then looked at me and smiled a wry smile, saying, "I understand and empathize with you. You know my father is a leading politician in Andhra Pradesh. He was very unhappy with me leaving the family business and politics and opting to do my MBA and then accept a job which took me away from the family."

He laughed. "I don't know what he will say when he finds out that I have finally found the girl I want to marry." I laughed with him, saying, "Bhavana is a lovely girl and your family will come around."

Prasanna smiled. "Let us look at your issue Krish, honestly you have no chance of getting the girl you believe you love, but you have a chance at happiness in your work."

"Take it. The girl you believe is your love may be an infatuation and you will get over it. No, don't protest or discuss that. Focus on your application. It is your life you need to take the call. There is an age limit, and if you keep dithering like this, you will be over age soon."

That night I thought long over what he had said. The Indian Navy Entrance Test was a mode of entry into the Indian Navy as an officer for graduates. I met all the qualifications required and was eligible to appear for the online test. It had an age limit of 25 years and in a couple of years, I would be ineligible because of overage. It was now or never, but I still hesitated.

The next day Sneha breezed into the office, waved at me and went out with Raghu. I realized then that continuing like this was not doing me any good and would only bring unhappiness all around. I needed to go away.

I remembered reading the novel "Beau Geste" by P. C. Wren about young men who join the French foreign legion to escape their troubles. I smiled to myself. Beau Geste, the tragic hero of the novel, always doing the right thing and sacrificing himself for others, was not me.

I would be rather be chasing my own dreams.

That night I filled up the application and the next day sent it.

Chapter fifteen

Sending of the application seemed to have released me and I felt more peaceful and calmer. My friends to observed the change. The next time we met, I looked at Bhavna and smiled. She blushed and turned to Prasanna, and he just nodded. Veena noticed the byplay, "Ah Kuzhanthai knows! You told him Prasanna."

"I don't need to be told I have eyes and am intelligent and don't call me that." I retorted. Veena sighed, "If only that was true." I looked at her, puzzled.

When I told them about sending the application, my friends were happy and Veena hugged me and I could see the glint of tears in her eyes.

Now that I had a definite goal which I wanted to achieve, I focused on it. I studied the syllabus, took mock tests, ate well and worked out more. The long jogs in the morning with Veena helped, and we developed an understanding. There was a change that everyone noticed. I was happier, calmer and did not worry about the work. I delegated more and found that this eased the pressure on me. Raghu had done a wonderful job of recruiting his people. We paid them well and treated them with respect and care. We had a couple of retired people from large organizations who were the backbone in the office.

The days flew by and I was content, if not happy. The day of the test, a Saturday, came around and I did well. I had a feeling that I could finally take the first step in achieving my dream.

We four of us went for a celebratory dinner that night, Prasanna, Bhavna, Veena and me. As we sat drinking our respective drinks, Prasanna his usual mocktail, we were a cheerful group with a lot of laughter. Veena did not call me Kuzhanthai even once, but she now had a new name for me: Popeye!

The others laughed at that, especially when she said it was not because of the cartoon Popeye the sailor, but because my eyes popped out!

Raghu walked in then with Sneha, saw us and came to our table. "Why all the merriment kids? What is the occasion?" he asked.

I was wondering what to say and was worried they would join us. Veena looked at Raghu mischievously. "Oh, it is just our age and our youthful spirits; you must have also remembered the fun you had when you were young?" Raghu looked at her and Veena kept her face innocent. Raghu was just a few years elder to us. He laughed. "Ok children, I know we will cramp your style, we will leave you alone."

They moved away, much to my relief, and I smiled at Veena. She patted my hand.

Prasanna had gone silent, and he looked at me. "Have you told your family?"

"No, I will tell them once I clear the SSB interview." I replied.

"I think you better tell them now, give them time to accept it, and also give time to Raghu to plan at work. If you wait till the last minute, it is unfair to your family. They will also feel hurt you told us and not them."

His words made sense, and I knew he was right. My family deserved me to be straight with them. I had always been a well-behaved boy, while Raghu had been the rebel.

That night when I went home, I decided to tell them the next day. Sunday, we normally ordered breakfast from the restaurant nearby, letting my mother have a relaxed day too. We sat together and ate together.

After we finished breakfast the next day, I told them I had given the Navy entrance exam and expected to clear it and I was also confident of clearing the SSB.

There was silence for a minute, then my mother said angrily, "no son of mine will join the armed forces." Before she could say anything, Raghu was standing up and looking at me. "I am surprised at you Krish, you should have checked with me before doing anything like this." Raghu turned to our father. "Did he check with you?"

My father calmed them both down, saying, "Let the boy be. He has just given the exam yesterday, and it is a long process. He has told us now so that we can help him prepare for the interview and also plan when he has to go." I looked at him with affection, saying "thank you for believing that I will clear both the exam and the interview and get selected."

Raghu exploded at that. "Are you an idiot, off course they will select you, there is no doubt of that; we know your capability. What will I do? I had big plans for us. Where will I find someone at such short notice?"

My father intervened. "Stop that. Let us support him." The rest of the day went with me explaining what the exam was about, what the job entailed and why I wanted to join. As I spoke, the clarity came in my mind and with that confidence in my voice.

It was with great reluctance that my mother and Raghu refrained from any further display of unhappiness.

The next day, a grim Raghu called me to his cabin. "I did not expect this of you, kid. You are leaving me in the lurch at a crucial moment. Please think again, consider the advantages of us working together, think about Amma and Appa, about me before you take any final decision."

Sometime later, Sneha came to meet Raghu and stopped at my cabin. "How can you do this, Krish? Did you not think of all of us who love you, your parents, your brother and your friends and how unhappy you are making all of us?"

I nodded my head with no emotion showing on my face. In all the discussions, other than my father, everyone seemed to talk about their love, happiness and need for me. No one had asked me what I wanted. In the afternoon Veena came, as usual, to have lunch with me and I unburdened myself to her. Her only response was to hold my hand and say, "don't let it worry you, take whatever decision makes you happy."

The atmosphere in the house and office was tense, but my father ensured they did not badger me and I coped with the disapproval. I was now clear in my mind what I wanted.

Chapter sixteen

The weeks went by, the results of the test came and I was through for the SSB interview. SSB stands for Service Selection Board, which is a body set up by the Indian Defense Ministry for interviewing candidates for selecting officers for the Indian Armed Forces.

I went to Bangalore for the SSB interview which is an arduous examination comprising intelligence and psychological testing. I felt good about myself for taking the first step in seeking my own path and happiness. My positivity seemed to rub off on the SSB members. My testing and interview were not the harrowing experience that many others had. We waited for the results, after which the successful candidate had to undergo a detailed medical and physical examination. Only after all this would the merit list be declared and you would know if they had selected you and you got the branch you wanted.

It was nerve-wracking sitting there with other hopefuls as we waited to know whether we had cleared the SSB interview. The selection process gave equal importance to the written tests and the interview. The medical and fitness test was also a detailed one.

They put the list of candidates who were selected to go further for the medical and fitness tests up. I had butterflies in my stomach and felt nausea and panic build up. I suppressed them, took a deep breath, and went to see the list. My name was on the list! I could hear my heart beat. I could hear the heartbeat of everyone! As I stumbled to a seat, I was floating in a mist of happiness.

Congratulations said my co candidates, and it was some time before I could relax enough to understand that I had cleared a major hurdle to my dreams. The medical and fitness test would be a difficult one, but I was now hopeful. I needed to talk to someone to clear my head. Prasanna was the obvious choice, but he was in a conference today and would probably not pick up the phone.

Almost without conscious effort, my hands found my phone and dialed the number of the person who had shared my dreams and walked, or rather ran, every step of the way with me.

Her phone rang, and she picked up, before I could say anything "hello dear dear Krish I am so so happy for you" she said and I could sense the genuine happiness in her voice.

"Thank you, Veena. It would not have been possible without you. I still have to clear the medical test, but yes, the SSB interview went well, and they have provisionally selected me subject to medical clearance." I spoke.

The names of the successful candidates were being called, and I said a quick goodbye, asking Veena not to tell anyone but Prasanna and Bhavna.

The medical and fitness tests took five days, and I was anxious. My friends called every evening and kept me sane. Other than my father, no one else from my family called.

They put up the final merit list, and I was high on the list. I had made it to my preferred choice, the Executive Service, or as it is termed now "the surface warfare division" of the Indian navy.

I walked out of the center. My induction into the training academy was still months away and the final commissioning was more than a year away. I was in euphoria and walking on air. The first person I called was Veena, and she screamed with joy at my news. Both Prasanna and Bhavana were with her. They were happy but more controlled in their reactions. Prasanna asked me if I had called my family. I had not, and he asked me to call them.

I did not want to speak to Raghu. We had a rather frosty relationship now, and he had not even wished me luck when I left. I called my father and told him I had found a place on the merit's top list. He laughed with genuine happiness "I knew you would clear the selection but to do it with such high a ranking under difficult circumstances shows your character, my son I am proud of you, don't worry, I am with you all the way."

I started off the next late afternoon after completing some more formalities and meeting a few friends. I was happier than I had been for a long time now. Little did I know the turbulence that awaited me back home.

Chapter seventeen

It was late at night when I reached back to Mysore to receive a cold welcome from brother and a weeping one from my mother. My father hugged me and I could sense his pride in me. Raghu just gave me a look and turned away; It hurt me.

In the morning, I found Raghu had left for the office without me. A further shock awaited me at the office. A new person was sitting in my chair and they had removed my name from my cabin. I had gone for only a week and Raghu had replaced me, saying nothing to me. I did not expect him to be so petty. I was mortified, hurt, and angry. The others in the office avoided looking at me.

I went into Raghu's office and he looked up at me with no expression. "Who is that in my room and am I fired? Could you not have the decency to at least tell me to my face and not go behind my back?" I asked in anger.

Raghu got up slowly, his face white with anger. "Go away Krish, you did not tell me before applying, leaving me in the lurch; why do you expect me to tell you what is my business?"

"I was employed here. You cannot remove me without even giving me notice. That is against our employee policy." I told him.

"I have not removed you, just demoted you from the Managing Director's position." He replied.

"Am I still on the board of directors, or have you voted me out?" I asked.

He looked down at his table, not meeting my eyes. "You are no longer on the board; we cannot have people I cannot trust. If you have any further queries, please check with the HR department. I am busy."

I stormed out of the office after throwing the keys of the car he had bought me on his table. There was utter silence outside as I strode out, tears blinded me. I dearly loved my brother. He had literally brought me up, protecting me, teaching me and pulling me out of many scrapes. He was the one to whom I went when I had problems, and he had rejected me so cruelly.

I went home and packed a bag. I felt I could no longer stay in the same house as Raghu. I did not tell my father or my mother, but slipped out without them knowing and started my bike. I was now determined that I would join the Navy. Earlier I had been in two minds and if Raghu had insisted that I not join, I would have listened to him. I had ingrained the habit of listening to him in me. But he had hurt me and I was upset. The matrix of obedience had changed.

I knew the paying guest accommodation where Prasanna stayed. It was a large building with many rooms and the manager knew me well. It was at Gokulam and when reached there the manager was there. A room was luckily available, but it was on the top floor next to the kitchen and dining area. I took the room and moved in. It was a large spacious room with an attached bath and had air conditioning.

In was late in the evening that a worried Prasanna came up to my room, the manager had informed him. He listened to the entire story in silence and then told me, "What you did was wrong. Your problem is with Raghu, but you have shown your anger and disrespect to your parents. You better go now and tell them. Tell them the truth. Tell them you need time to process this new situation."

I was ashamed and agreed to go home and tell my parents, but I was adamant I would stay here as I did not want to face Raghu.

I reached home and found my father angry and facing Raghu. My mother was weeping. They all turned to me and my father moved a quick step towards me. "How dare you do this, Krish? Leave the house like this telling none of us?"

I stammered out an apology. "I am sorry. I was hurt and angry with Raghu and should not have taken it out on both of you."

Raghu looked at me but remained silent. My father took a deep breath and calmed himself and spoke.

"Tell me what happened."

"Raghu has fired me and removed me from the board of directors. He has not informed me in advance, not given me any notice and humiliated me in the office. He has appointed someone without even checking with me."

"You went and applied to join the Navy without informing me, leaving me in the lurch, after all that I have done for me. You are ungrateful, Krish," said Raghu.

"I have to join only after 4 months and I have not yet confirmed my acceptance. I wanted to discuss with you and father and then take a decision. And yes, I am grateful to you but you also should appreciate me. I have taken up the slack for you and done work which no paid employee would have done. I have not slacked off and earned every rupee that you have spent on me. After all that, to treat me so badly and humiliate me in front of everyone was very hurting to me."

Raghu calmed down. "You have not accepted?"

"No, I have not." I replied.

"Good, tomorrow I will reinstate you in a senior position." Smiled Raghu.

"Did you even listen to what I said? You only focus on what you want. No, I am not coming back. What guarantee is there that you will not do the same thing again later?" I asked.

Raghu looked embarrassed and angry, too. "You know me kid, I get angry and do and say things which I don't mean. Forget what happened, come tomorrow and we will set everything right."

I shook my head, and as Raghu tried to speak, my father intervened. "Let us call it a day. Let tempers cool. We will discuss this tomorrow. Go to your rooms now."

We were still kids to him and he expected obedience. Indian parents are like that.

Raghu turned to go, but I did not go. "I have taken a room at a PG (Paying Guest accommodation). I think I will stay there. It will avoid unpleasantness." I said.

My father looked at me silently. "You have grown, my son. Go but come back tomorrow" He nodded to me.

Raghu turned to me, anger and astonishment in his eyes. He had never seen me disobey him or my parents till then; I was the ideal son. But he said nothing but watch me get up on my bike.

Chapter eighteen

I went home in the morning but refused any attempts to get me back at the house or the office.

Raghu seemed to have accepted that I would not immediately go back. He told me, "Look Kid, I am sorry, I lost my temper and was unfair to you. Take your time, take a break, think about what we both can do together. I have plans to build one of the biggest logistics companies in the region and we can do it. No, don't give me an answer now. Take your time."

He ruffled my head as he left. It was the old Raghu, my elder brother, who took care of me, protected me and exacted instant obedience from me. From childhood, I had followed him around and obeyed him in everything. If I had a problem, I went to him and he solved it. I discussed everything with him and my decisions were what he advised.

But I had changed now. I felt good about myself. It was time to leave the nest, time to assert my independence. But this was not the right time to discuss this with Raghu, and I kept silent. My father looked at me, his eyes on my face, and I faced his scrutiny without flinching.

He turned back to his plate with a smile. That encouraged me and I felt comforted that I had his support.

Later, he sat with me and the first thing he said was, "It feels good to know that my little son has grown up enough to seek his own happiness. You have a lot of potential and need to find your own way."

We discussed everything, and my father was a sensible person with a lot of good advice. He also was patient and never pushed his own views on me. I normally discussed little with him. I was more of a mama's boy and discussed any problems or career issues with Raghu.

The outcome of our discussion was that I would continue to stay at the PG. My father and I would manage our estate and farm. I would make a summary of all the work I had done, make a proper account of the work and finance, return the laptops etc. to Raghu.

I would make an account of all my assets and leave a copy with my father. If I required any money, he would let me have it. I smiled at that. Raghu had been paying me a very good salary, and I had little expenses. I had saved enough and that would tide me over till I joined and drew my first salary from the Navy.

I sent my acceptance letter to the Navy and received details of joining, where to report, what to carry, and such details.

But we make plans and they change, the next day saw one of father's old friends, Uncle Joe, from Kerala came home. He was one of the best-known designers and tuners for race cars and rally cars in India. He had a branch in Mysore and as there was a gravel rally scheduled to be held in Mysore; he had come personally to check out the course and get his customer's vehicle ready. The main agenda for him was to attend the rally. Many of his customers were taking part, of course, and he also enjoyed rallies and racing. He was a man who chased his dreams even at this age.

He saw my bike outside and was curious about it and when he heard I had rebuilt it; it impressed him. "Why don't you join me, son? I need talented engineers, and anyone who can do what you did is a genuine talent."

I laughed. "No uncle, they have selected me for the Indian Navy and I will leave for my training in a few months. But I am free for the next few months and if you want a hand to cope with the work for the Rally, I will be happy to join you."

We quickly settled it. I would go the next day, learn the ropes and assist in the work.

Chapter nineteen

The next day, I reported to their center. Any idea I had that this was a mechanic shop quickly disappeared. It was a place which modified and provided aftermarket services. They did tune and modify vehicles for racing. But the principal business was designing modifications to vehicles, designing luxury buses, campers and caravans. The office had gleaming machines; people were on computer screens checking out data. The workshop had machines which scanned the vehicles and let us know its status. The workshop itself was large, well ventilated, and clean.

There were cars being readied for the Rally. It was a gravel rally so the course would have rough patches, dust, dirt, water, ramps and jumps. This meant not only that the engine needed to be tuned to perfection but also that the suspension needed to be worked on ensuring the vehicles would last the course.

When I turned up on my 1976 Norton Commando, it created a stir. This was a rare motor cycle they made only about 60000 numbers. Norton had a racing pedigree, and this was an iconic motorcycle, the last model the company made before it folded. The company was revived in 2008 and in 2020 TVS had taken over it.

When the others heard I had rebuilt the bike all by myself, they became friendly. Most of the people there had other work they did for a living, working on vehicle and rallying was a hobby. These were the interns who worked for a short time specifically for the rally.

I quickly picked up the work, and it was fun to be among so many young people of my age. When they learned my background, they were intrigued and congratulated me on following my heart in joining the Navy.

The situation at the home front worsened. Raghu always tried to get me to discuss when I would come back. He kept offering me incentives to join him. I refused. One day, he lost his temper and shouted at me, calling me an ungrateful wretch. I got up in anger and left the room. My father spoke to Raghu and asked him to stop asking me to come back and let me find my own way.

Raghu stopped talking to me and then avoiding or ignoring me completely. My mother had tried to get me to change my mind. She cajoled, threatened, tried to make me feel guilty, but I stood firm. My father was an enormous support, and he soothed my mother and got her to accept my choice.

Mysore is a small town and, though it has grown because of its proximity to Bangalore, it still keeps its small-town ethos and habits.

Our family was well known and soon the differences between me and Raghu was common knowledge. In typical small-town fashion, many acquittances called up to find out the reason. My father put it about that I was selected for the Navy and during the four-month gap period I wanted to relax and hence was pursuing my hobby.

But people knew there was a problem. When we met at a restaurant or at a function, Raghu and I avoided each other.

I rarely saw Sneha and had not exchanged words since she had spoken to me that day in the office. She turned up at the workshop one day and asked to see me. I was reluctant, but could not refuse.

She had come to plead Raghu's case; not check how I was or wish me for being selected.

Sneha said "Krish you are a good friend and Raghu is very dear to me. I hate to see you both estranged like this. Come back and Raghu will reinstate you as the Managing Director or he will do whatever you want. He is miserable without you and sorry for the way he behaved. Raghu may not show it, but he misses you and cannot focus on his work. The man is worried about you."

I shrugged my shoulders; my anger and sense of loss burned me up, but I kept a resolute face.

"I miss him too. He is my brother. I expected and wanted him to help me chase my dream, not force me to work for his." I replied harshly, "you call me a friend, but you never spoke to me all these months, you never wished me for the selection, you did not even ask me how I was, Sneha. Now you come around and want me to go back to doing something in which I have no interest. No Sneha, this will not work. Don't do Raghu's dirty work for him."

Sneha's face became white with anger. "Raghu was right. You are an ungrateful wretch. I am sorry I considered you as my friend." She raged at me, turned on her heel, and left. I was angry with myself and also with Sneha and Raghu for trying to manipulate me.

I went to work on one of the old Baleno sedans that was now to be tuned. The Baleno is a wonderful car with one of the best drivetrains and very driver friendly, but its fuel intake was throttled down to improve mileage. It was interesting to see how minor changes improved performance in many vehicles. I forced myself to focus and tried to forget my heartbreak. The work helped.

Evening brought further misery, Raghu flared up at the dinner table over my rudeness to Sneha and I could bear it no longer, my fury and frustration at the situation boiled over and I called him to task for betraying the family and washing dirty linen in public by discussing it with outsiders. I told him he had stabbed me in the back repeatedly and I owed him nothing.

Raghu was drinking water to calm himself down. My words worked him up, and in his fury, he threw his glass at me. It hit me on my forehead, shattered and cut me just above my eyebrow. It was a minor cut but any cut there bleeds a lot and in seconds my face was bloody and blood dripped onto my plate.

Raghu was aghast and contrite, and I was shocked and angry. It was a chance to show him up, was the petty thought in my head. I stood up and glared at him "you have taken advantage of being elder to me all the time, made me work against my wishes, threw me out when you did not need me anymore and now assault me when you know I will not retaliate, you are a cad and coward Raghu."

Raghu's face was ashen. He moved towards me with a pleading look, but my father stopped him.

"Raghu, go to your room. You have done enough mischief tonight. Krish will keep silent."

My mother had been to the kitchen to get something and came into the room hearing the commotion. She screamed when she saw my face and rushed to me, but my father waved her away, asking her to get some clean cloth and hot water and Dettol. He cleaned my face and sighed with relief. "It is a minor cut, not much damage, but for the bleeding to stop, it needs to be stitched."

We went to the nearby hospital, a small one where everyone knew us. My father told the doctor the truth and asked him to not spread it. The doctor stitched the small would and put a tape over it. We told everyone who asked that I had a minor accident on my bike.

By morning, it was the talk in the social circles of how Raghu had beaten me up. The story got added in each retelling and by evening it had grown to such proportions that an evening daily carried it without mentioning names. It said a big businessman had assaulted his younger brother because of differences in business!

Many of our friends laughed. They knew part of the truth. But neither me nor Raghu nor our family could laugh it off.

Veena, when she met me during lunch, was nearly in tears when I told her the whole story. She patted me repeatedly and soon Prasanna, Bhavana and Govind joined us. Their concern touched me. Govind told me Sneha seemed upset and spoke little to anyone in the office. My friends seemed to blame Sneha for coming between brothers.

Sneha called me, but I ignored her calls and did not return the calls. She gave up after sometime. I heard later she had tried to talk to my friends but had been rebuffed by Veena and Bhavna. Prasanna spoke to her and told her to be patient and he would try to reconcile me and Raghu.

My father came to the workshop. He was upset at what had happened. He called Raghu, and we went to the farm where there would be no one but us.

Raghu was silent until we reached the farm. The minute we reached he hugged me and held me tight. "I am very sorry, kid; I don't know what happened and how it happened. Believe me, I would not hurt you for anything in this world. I don't know how to make things all right between us. Please forgive me."

I hugged him back and both of us were crying.

My father let us get our emotions under control. He smiled. "I am glad that is out of the way." But we cannot go on like this. There are bound to be misunderstandings. We need to ensure this does not happen again.

Both of us nodded and Raghu promised he would not try to force me to join him, but he still wanted me to come back.

We went back together to our home. My mother refused to let us enter until she removed the evil eye on us. As far as she was concerned, her sons could do no wrong and someone felt envious and put their evil eye on us.

Dinner that night was a cheerful affair, me and Raghu were on our best behavior. The violence and blood seemed to have brought both of us to our senses.

Chapter twenty

The peace between us lasted nearly a fortnight and then flared up again. Raghu was finding it difficult to manage his expansion and never seemed to have any time. He made a few attempts to discuss with me and get me back with him, but I refused to even talk about it.

He finally gave up and stopped talking with me. I saw him a few times with Sneha, but we avoided each other as much as possible and behaved like strangers. Sneha too avoided me and pretended to not know me when we met in public.

Raghu had been practicing rallying in his Mahindra Thar, the new four-wheel-drive vehicle he had bought recently. He brought it in for some minor modifications and they allotted it to me.

I did the modifications, and he took it in the evening for a test drive. I was in the next room when he came back and expressed his unhappiness at the work done. "Why do you keep untrained kids around to attend to expensive vehicles like this? It is dangerous and not safe. Get rid of him." I heard Raghu say.

Uncle Joe was angry. "All my boys are responsible and good, come let us jointly go for a test drive on the trial course." They returned with Uncle Joe lecturing Raghu about being careful in accusing someone. "As you saw, Raghu, there was nothing wrong with the work done. The problem was with your driving. When you try to drift around a corner, you need to be faster on the steering. You saw I had no issues when I drove. There was adequate power, and the tuning was good. You also need to remember that your vehicle has a different center of gravity than a standard car. Any mistake can see you topple over."

I came out then and said angrily, "Thank you, uncle Joe, for supporting me. Raghu just wants to show me up. He does not want me to be happy." Raghu snorted, turned, and left.

That night at dinner, Raghu was absent, and my father took me to task. "Raghu did not know that you had worked on his vehicle, and he has never publicly said anything about the differences between you two. Why did you blame him publicly, Krish?" I had no answer.

The break between us widened with this. Raghu stopped talking to me and ignored me when we were forced to meet in a public place. Others noticed the difference and people started taking sides. Most of Raghu's friends too stopped talking to me. I stopped taking calls from many of our relatives. My mother was mortified, but my father remained calm.

Among my friends, Prasanna still kept in touch with Raghu and would often try to get me to call Raghu.

Sneha and the girls too stopped talking to each other and the fissure between us brothers was observed and commented on frequently. After a couple of weeks, the story died down as people accepted the situation.

The rally was to be held on the grounds of the Lalitha Mahal Palace; I checked out the course.

I often rode my Norton on the course and was soon familiar with it.

Joe's uncle observed me and asked me one day, "why don't you take part in the rally meant for bikes? You ride well, your bike is in excellent condition, and the Norton frame is still one of the best. A gravel rally is not just about speed, try it."

I hesitated there would be some of the latest bikes and I stood no chance I felt. Uncle Joe would have none of it. "Think of it as a fun ride, take part as an experience, not to win."

We went back to the workshop and uncle Joe worked his magic on the bike. It surprised me to see he made slight adjustments to the engine placement. We tried the handling and finally found the sweet spot where we both felt the improvement in handling. The suspension was checked, especially the rubber bushes which had a tendency to wear out. A worn-out bush could lead to fishtailing at high-speed and a crash.

There was a devil may attitude in me and I had time to spare. I rode the bike flat out over the course, taking risks I normally would not. I felt free. Uncle Joe came along with me and he taught me many tricks of rallying. I absorbed his teachings and improved day by day.

Chapter twenty one

The day of the rally came and there was dust, the roar of exhausts, noise, chaos, clatter and crowds.

I had a privileged place as a participant and one of Joe's teams. I would ride my race as part of their team. Neither my friends nor family knew I was also taking part in a race. The rally was not racing but more of time trials. Batches of vehicles of a particular class would complete the course and timings would be recorded. The winner would be based on the best time overall. The fastest lap also would have a prize.

The bikes of the heavier class lined up, and it amazed everyone when I rolled up on my vintage bike. I could see the worry on my family's faces. Raghu was there with Sneha and when he saw me, he rushed up to me. I could sense the genuine fear and worry on his face. He had forgotten all our differences. All he saw was his younger brother was about to do something dangerous.

"Krish, wait, are you mad? You cannot take part in such a dangerous race on that old bike of yours."

Prasanna, who represented the main sponsor, came up then equally worried and supported Raghu.

Uncle Joe told them they need not worry. He had checked the bike, and it was fine. I laughed at my brother and friend. "Wish me luck you two, don't worry, I won't do anything rash. All I want is to complete the course."

Raghu hugged me hard. "Good luck, kid, make us proud." He whispered.

The other riders admired my classic bike but felt it was not much of a threat. We roared off when the flag was down.

The hours of practice and uncle Joe's lessons helped, the weight and balance of my vehicle also helped. Most others were riding vehicles, which they used only for rallying. Many of the vehicles did not even belong to them and they were not familiar with the vehicle.

I was familiar with my bike and the course. I had no intention of winning or getting placed, there was no pressure on me. There were also the months of pent-up frustration and anger. It was time to let go.

Most of the other bikes were ahead of me in the straight speed section. The first sharp turn came up, and I took it at full speed. The improved handling helped, and I was now ahead of many. On the straights they caught up but, on the turns, the water section or the ramps and other obstacles, my familiarity with the course and bike made a difference. The frustrations and the anger of months were now channeled into this ride.

I was one with the bike; it seemed to share my mood of happiness and the urge to prove myself equal to the others. I was in the zone; I forgot the others, my troubles and everything. There was only me and the bike and the course. We roared through corners and jumped from the ramps. The water section was fun and suddenly there was the flag on the last lap.

I roared through the last lap at full speed, never slowing down at the corners. I could barely hear the noise of the crowd and suddenly the finish line was there. I crossed the line and slowed down to a stop. The noise of the crowd hit me when I removed my helmet.

Uncle Joe was there smiling, Raghu and Prasanna with wide smiles but also disbelief on their faces. The other riders came up then, congratulating me and slapping on the back and shaking their head.

"What happened?" I asked. Uncle Joe held me by my shoulders. "You did the impossible, you came third, you have a place. You beat many of the latest machines and some of the best riders on your vintage bike." He laughed.

I could not believe it and walked around in a daze. "Come and watch me race," said Raghu, and I watched as he roared around the course. I had a secret hope that Raghu would also get placed, but that was not to be. His inexperience showed in the turns and he came somewhere at the back.

We met together at the participant's enclosure and he grinned at me and it was the old Raghu. The speed and thrill of racing and shared danger made us forget our differences.

We walked together hand in hand to where our family and friends waited. I could sense the happiness and relief in my parents' eyes. Prasanna had a smile for me. Veena made as if to throw herself at me, but restrained herself to a quick hug. Sneha looked worried and uncomfortable, but I smiled at her and there was peace between us.

The prize distribution was a fun affair, and it surprised me to see Prasanna was the chief guest who would hand over the prizes. He grinned at me as he handed over my small trophy and the cheque for the third place.

As my family and friends made much of my placing, Raghu came up with the idea that I should turn professional. "Give up this silly Indian Navy stuff, become a professional rider and you can work with me in your spare time." I considered it for a minute till Joe brought us down to reality.

"He got placed today as the competition was weak. This is the first gravel rally in Mysore and has not yet picked up. Also, Krish had beginner's luck that he did not fall on any of the turns. He was taking them much too fast. Modern racing or rallying requires a lot of money, training and effort, Krish is already too old. People start when they are 18 or 19." Uncle Joe laughed at my woebegone face. He clapped me on the shoulder. "Well done, but keep it as a hobby."

I laughed and shook my head. "It is the Navy for me".

The remaining days went in a flurry of preparation for my departure for training. The relationship between me and Raghu remained cordial, but the earlier closeness was missing. I spent more time with Prasanna and the girls. We were always together. I put up a happy façade to the world, but there was a well of sadness in me. I still felt the tug on my heartstrings when I saw Sneha and when I saw her with Raghu, it was almost unbearable sometimes. It was good I was going away. It was now clear that they had cleared up their differences, and it was only a matter of time before they got married.

The day of departure came. I was joining the training school at Ezhimala in the Kannur District in Kerala for my basic training. It was just a five-hour drive from Mysore. I expected Raghu would drive me to the school and my parents would come. But a distance had grown between us.

Raghu neither asked me when I was leaving nor offered to drive me. My friends took a quick break and drove me to the school.

We left on an early morning a few days before I was to join. My parents came to see us off. I searched for Raghu but could not find him. "Raghu had to go to Mumbai for some work. He asked me to convey his regards and love to you," said my father.

My heart ached at the break from family. I had lost not only Sneha but my brother as well. It was a double heartbreak.

The portals of the Indian Naval Academy opened before me and I stepped into a new life.

Epilogue

I sat thinking about my life before I joined the academy. On my commissioning, only my father and Prasanna, Bhavana and Veena had come. I kept in touch through the occasional call and messages. Veena regularly called me, but Raghu had never called nor had Sneha. I spoke to my parents when I could. The oceans were between me and my loved ones. Over time, I got over my heartbreak and learned to smile and laugh wholeheartedly.

My friends at the academy and the navy called me an old confirmed bachelor. I never seemed interested in any of the ladies we met. I kept myself aloof and seemed content to focus wholly on my job.

There was the bump of the aircraft landing, and it jolted me out of my thoughts. We had arrived in Delhi.

I reported to the commanding officer of the Naval Expedition. We quickly completed the formalities.

"Krish, you need not rush off to Cochin. There has been a delay in the Antarctic expedition and it has been postponed by six months, something to do with ministry clearance. We have plenty of time. Take a few days off. You may not get the chance again for a couple of years." Said my commanding officer.

It was a message from the universe; I thought wryly. I had no excuse now to avoid going to Mysore. I took leave and left for Mysore.

I wanted to surprise everyone and so had informed no one of my coming. It was late evening when I reached and checked into the Radisson Blu hotel. The marriage was to be in the hotel's ballroom.

I went down for dinner and was walking across to the dining area. There were some new people arriving. I heard a scream and turned towards the entrance and someone flung themselves into my arms. It was a young woman who was holding me tight and laughing and crying at the same time.

I knew the voice saying Krish, Krish and knew only one person who would rub her nose and face on my clothes like this. I held her tight, laughing, and Veena looked up at me with wonder and joy.

Prasanna came behind her, a big grin on his face.

We sat up late that night. Bhavana was to come from Gujarat the next day morning. The next day went in a flash and in the evening, I dressed up for the Mehndi function, which would start of the celebrations.

I stood at the entrance of the hall and bit hesitant to face the ghosts of the past. A soft hand slipped into mine and I looked into Veena's eyes, so full of love.

My heart stirred, and I was on the road to redemption.

But that is a story for another time.

Also by R RADHAKRISHNAN

The Mysore Triology
A Road less travelled

The Temples of India
The Temples of India: Somnathapura, Mysore

Travellers Tales
Rustic Romeo

Standalone
The Colors of Life
The Temples of India : Guruvayur
Indian Mythology
The Book of Ancient Wisdom
Karna's Song
Artificial intelligence : AI for writers

About the Author

Radhakrishnan, a seasoned traveler and storyteller, hails from Mumbai, India, and has explored various parts of the country during his three-decade-long career in a petroleum company. Being fluent in six languages has enabled him to connect with people and listen to their stories.

Passionate about narratives, Radhakrishnan has been exposed to a wide range of stories and their different versions throughout his travels, which significantly transformed his perspectives on life and India as a whole. His book, "Traveller's Tales Once upon a Time," set in the rapidly changing India of the 1970s, 1980s, and 1990s, offers captivating insights into a bygone era. With a delightful touch of humor and profound insight, these stories are sure to captivate and enchant readers.

Radhakrishnan's fascination with Indian mythology has led him to immerse himself in the ancient tales that have been passed down through generations. He heard these stories first from his parents and grandparents and later during encounters with many people during his journeys. These timeless stories embody the essence of India's soul, forming a living mythology in the ancient land. Radhakrishnan masterfully retells these tales, infusing simplicity and clarity while highlighting the invaluable life lessons they impart, lessons that remain relevant in the present day.

After retiring from Indian Oil, Radhakrishnan now dedicates his time fully to his passion for writing and traveling. His writing style is marked by simplicity, clarity, and empathy, effortlessly presenting complex ideas in concise and understandable ways. Occasionally, his emotions spill over, giving rise to stark and minimalist poetry, where profound thoughts and ideas are beautifully etched.

When not exploring India, Radhakrishnan lives in the picturesque coastal city of Cochin, Kerala, with his wife and two children. He maintains a blog titled **radhawrites.com**. Experience the artistry of Radhakrishnan's storytelling and embark on a journey through his vivid narratives, allowing yourself to be transported to the heart of India's diverse tapestry.

Read more at https://radhawrites.com.